I0586979

# Feelings in Staccato
## The book of stories

MARIA GRIGORESCU

ISBN-13: 978-0-6452302-6-0 (Paperback)

*This is a work of fiction. Unless otherwise indicated, all the
names, characters, businesses, places, events and incidents in
this book are either the product of the author's imagination or
used in a fictitious manner. Any resemblance to actual persons,
living or dead, or actual events is purely coincidental.*

Front cover photo by Raul Popa (2021)
Painting by Cristina Grigorescu, "Decizii" – "*Decisions*",
(Acrylic on canvas, 2021)
Book cover design by The Illustrators (theillustrators.com.au)
Photography by Les Moyle (2022)
Second edition 2022
Instagram: mariagrigorescu_

For Raduca and Raul:

*Never stop dreaming.*

# CONTENTS

# INTRODUCTION BY R. GRIGORESCU

Much like everywhere else in the world, Romanian fairy tales start with a formulaic expression, roughly translated like this:

> *There once was, as never before –*
> *because if there wasn't, we wouldn't tell*
> *stories about it –  ...*

And then the story goes on: *There once was, as never before, a beautiful girl.* Or: *There once was, because we wouldn't tell this story if there wasn't, a brave young man and his talking horse.*

It's an expression so ingrained in our culture that I often say it to myself when I start to read works of fiction even now, fifteen years after leaving Romania. It provides a sort of settling down, an escape from reality and an entry into a specific mind space where I don't have to think about what I'm reading – I only need to sit and let someone tell me a story.

For as long as I've been able to communicate and understand stories, it's also a feeling I've had whenever my mother told me stories. She wasn't much the fairy tale type – but then, she didn't need to be. I avidly read and reread fairy tales from small paperbacks and bulky hardcover books until the bindings on them frayed and fell apart. No, my mother instilled the love of stories in me by telling me her own stories, which were so far removed from my own experiences that they seemed as though they happened on another planet – or in a fairy tale.

These were stories from her own life, about growing up under communism, about our family's history, about people she had met and known and loved. Some stories were sad, some were happy; some were told to me at important parts of my life, when I needed advice and support. Some stories may even be in this collection, or they may not. But for as long as I've been able to listen to stories, she has always had one for me.

And even as I was growing up, she was always writing. I remember typewritten manuscripts and handwritten journals and, always, the feeling that I wanted to know what stories she found worth telling. I suppose now I finally have my answer, because I was involved with the making of this short story collection at various steps, usually as my mother's first reviewer. I'm in the unique and happy position of knowing exactly from which seed every story has sprouted, and I could not be any prouder of what an achievement this collection is.

I only hope that everyone who will ever read these stories will be as enraptured by these stories as I am when I read them, that they will be transported from the mundane to the extraordinary. I hope that everyone gets that fairy tale feeling.

To help with that, let me reiterate:

*There once was, as never before…*

# AUNT MARY

Do you remember my silver handbag?'
The voice startled Joan and she dropped the pot into the soapy water.

'Aunt Mary! Why didn't you tell me you were coming?'

Her aunt smiled from the doorway and Joan watched her curiously.

'Do you remember the handbag or not?'

'Well, yes, of course. I called it the Gatsby bag. Give me a second to rinse my hands.'

The sink drains gurgled.

'Do you remember the shell-covered box?'

Joan rinsed the foam off the sink.

'Such an ugly box. Yes, I remember it.' Joan took in the frail figure in the summer dress — blue with yellow flowers, one of her aunt's favourites. 'You sound tired, Aunty Mary.'

'The handbag is in my underwear drawer and the shell box is in the attic.'

'What is this about, Aunty?' Joan dried her hands. 'I'll make a nice fluffy latte, the way you like it, and we'll talk.' She scooped some coffee beans into the machine.

'Get the handbag and the box. The key for the box is in the handbag. You must find the ring.'

Joan threw a glance over her shoulder.

'What are you talking about?'

'You'll have to go very soon.'

'You're not making any sense, Aunt Mary.' Joan turned, but her aunt had already left the kitchen. 'Where are you?'

Joan walked down the hallway, searched in the living room, then went into the bedroom, but she couldn't find her aunt. She kept looking around the house and out on the porch. There was no sign of Aunt Mary. She ran her fingers through her short hair.

'You are very mysterious, Aunt Mary. Why are you doing this to me?'

The well-known violet scent of her aunt's perfume lingered in the kitchen. Joan decided to call her cousin Charlotte. As if on cue, the phone rang.

'Charlotte! I was just about to call you.'

Her cousin sobbed.

'Charlotte! What is it?'

'My mother … your Aunt Mary … is dead.'

'What? It can't be! I just spoke—' Joan fell silent. Her stomach dropped and her hand rubbed the crawls on her neck.

'Her neighbour found her this morning and called the

ambulance,' her cousin said.

Charlotte carried on talking about neighbours, the family, and the funeral arrangements.

'Wait! What actually happened?'

'The paramedic said it was a heart attack. I just spoke to the funeral home, and they will bring her home tonight. Will you come to help?'

What had her aunt said? That Joan would have to go very soon.

Charlotte whimpered. 'You must come and keep the wake with me.'

'So, she died alone? Was she in pain?'

'I don't think so. They think she died in her sleep. But in the past month she'd been difficult. She had started to forget things.'

'You should have said something.'

'That's easy for you to say.' Charlotte sobbed some more. 'Please come. I don't want to be alone with her in the house.'

The clock above the door ticked its seconds.

'I need to take care of a few things. I will be with you this evening, okay?'

Charlotte hung up, leaving Joan to speak to the walls. 'What on earth is going on? How come you were here, Aunty? Were you here?'

For the next few hours, Joan scrambled around the house in a haze. She packed a small bag with a change of black clothes, and she lost track of time while recalling her aunt's words and picturing her in the flowery dress. She called work to take a few days off, had a shower and dressed in black jeans and a pullover. Their conservative family would expect a proper mourning.

Joan drove for more than three hours. When she arrived, the light was on above the entrance. As soon as she entered the house, Charlotte took her bag, pushed her into the dining room and left her on her own.

3

Chairs were pushed against the wall and windows were covered by thick curtains. A trestle table stood alone in the middle of the room. It was covered to the floor with a white tablecloth and the coffin was placed on it. The coffin, in dark chocolate carved wood, had two half lids. The body was accessible for viewing only from the waist up. The room was lit by candles and the thickest of them were placed on each side of the coffin. The yellow light accentuated the bad makeup. Her aunt had had a professional do — eyeshadow, blush, liner — like she had never had in her life. She looked cheery, maybe a bit too cheery, with her pink cheeks. Her mouth was sunken in, her white hair combed back but for a few strands left wild on her forehead which gave her a youngish look. Aunt Mary was dressed in the blue dress with big yellow sunflowers, the very same dress she had had on earlier in Joan's kitchen. Aunt Mary was clearly dead then.

Joan touched her aunt's face. It was cold and the makeup felt greasy. She wanted to feel pain; she wanted to cry. Her own mother had died when she was only twelve and her father did everything in his power to be both mother and father. Joan spent lots of time with his sister, Aunt Mary. As a teenager, Joan had cried on Aunt Mary's lap when her first boyfriend dumped her, they planned family gatherings together, her aunt helped her get her first big job and loaned her money for her first car. Joan pinched herself hard and shut her eyes tight, hoping to squeeze out a tear or two. She coughed to imitate Charlotte's sob. All in vain.

Her cousin returned, holding a handkerchief to her nose. She saw Joan's tense face and hugged her. 'Oh, poor you. You cannot cry. Oh, my dear. She is really gone. So many holidays and birthdays when her cakes will be missed.'

'Well, we'll have to find a cake maker,' Joan said.

There was a knock at the front door and Charlotte left

again.

'Well, Aunty Mary, you really did it this time, didn't you?'

'It was not planned, my dear. Not planned at all.'

Joan recoiled and took a step away from the coffin, but then curiosity won. She went closer to examine her aunt's face.

'You are looking in the wrong place.'

Joan looked around and found her aunt standing beside her. The scent of violets again. Joan looked from her aunt to her right to the body in the coffin. Her aunt's body and clothes were see-through. Joan distanced herself from the apparition.

Aunt Mary ignored her behaviour. 'We don't have time. You need to do what I asked you.'

'If this is a game, I am not enjoying it.'

Aunt Mary spoke in a hushed voice, as if afraid to disturb the dead body in the coffin. 'Shhh, stop being a child. Just do what I asked you. You've got to find the ring. I promised your uncle just before he died. He asked for the ring every hour of his last days.' With a feeble gesture of her hand, she dismissed a thought. 'I fell ill, and I forgot, and I did not know how to find it.' Then her face suddenly looked energised. 'But you can!'

With one finger, Joan poked her aunt's cheek. Her finger, followed by her hand, passed through and the air was chilled. Aunt Mary chuckled; the laugh made her body sway gently.

'Let me know when you're finished playing.'

Joan remained silent, retreated to the back wall and sat. The apparition produced herself on the chair next to her.

'I told you I was going to haunt you if you did not eat your greens, and you did not eat your greens. So, here I am.' Aunt Mary's attempt to lighten the mood was without success. 'Joan, come to your senses. I need you to do what I asked.'

'Come to my senses? Are you kidding me? What senses are we talking about?'

Her aunt's eyes glimmered with a smile as she waved her hands over her body.

'Stop doubting what you see. We are wasting time. If you do what I tell you, you will find proof and then you will accept I am here. Can you follow my logic?'

Joan nodded at her transparent aunt.

'I cannot just go and search in your drawers and in the attic. Charlotte will think I am trying to steal something.'

'Charlotte would, wouldn't she? But you are a smart girl. You will find a way.'

'I … I can't.'

Joan was standing, ready to leave, when Charlotte returned.

'People are arriving for the wake. I get nervous when there are so many people. You should go and talk to them. I will stay with her now.' Charlotte was opening the door for Joan when a strong wind started to stir the curtains and the tablecloth beneath the coffin. The door slammed shut.

Charlotte whimpered. 'What is happening? It's like she doesn't want you to leave.'

Joan mimicked her. 'Oh no! The ghost of Aunt Mary keeps me here!'

Wide-eyed, her cousin said, between sobs, 'You always were her favourite and now you are mocking me.'

'Stop it, Charlotte. It was just a draught.'

'What draught? The windows are shut.'

Another wind started to stir; when Joan tried the doorknob, the door resisted. The wind swished around her. She could not fight with imaginary winds.

'Where did you take my bag? I hope I'm not sleeping in the bedroom where she died.'

Charlotte rolled her eyes. 'It is the only room available.'

'Then I guess I don't have a choice,' Joan said, both

for Charlotte and her aunt.

The wind subsided, and the door opened by itself.

As Joan stepped out of the room, her aunt's voice trailed after her. 'By the way, you must do something about my makeup. I look like a tramp! Do me a favour and get somebody to wipe this muck off my face. Your cousin couldn't care less. And get them to find my dentures. I was the one with dementia, not them.'

Charlotte continued to stare blankly at the coffin. Joan ran out of the room to hide her smile. The ghost was indeed her aunt, she was now convinced.

Her aunt's bedroom looked untidy. A few drawers were pulled out, and the vanity dresser was a mess. Joan found the Gatsby handbag in a drawer and the key in a tiny side pocket. She was glad that no one else was upstairs to see her sneak into the attic and snoop around for the ugly seashell box. She found it among other holiday souvenirs stacked in a basket. Joan felt compelled to unlock the box away from the dead lady dressed in sunflowers. There was only a pile of letters tied with a ribbon. She hid them under her pullover then returned downstairs. The house was abuzz with people coming to pay their respects.

For the next few days, they would bring homemade food to eat together. They'd drink strong alcohol and pour a few drops on the floor for Mary's sips. Mary was a well-loved woman with lots of friends. They wanted to show their love and respect with a proper wake, where family and friends would reminisce about her life. The time left with her was short and they would make the most of it.

'The dementia was quite advanced in recent months. She could never remember when she saw me last,' one of Joan's cousins said.

Joan hugged him. 'I am so sorry for our loss, Ronnie.'

'Yeah, me too. Have you seen her?'

Joan nodded. 'She looks so … painted.'

The mess in Aunt Mary's room extended to the rest of the house as well. The sitting room was crowded with opened boxes, books were off the shelves, and the china cabinet looked as if it had been rearranged as the cups did not fit the old dust marks.

'What happened here?' Joan asked.

One of the neighbours answered. 'Charlotte told me she was looking for something. I guess with all this happening she never got to tidy things up.'

'What was she looking for?'

'She said she lost a ring.'

Ronnie took the opportunity. 'The precious!'. They all laughed at the *Lord of the Rings* reference and drizzled drops of brandy on the floor to include Mary in their joke.

The neighbour continued. 'Your uncle lost your aunt's wedding ring a few years back. He always felt so bad about it. They couldn't find it anywhere.'

This information made Joan think a bit more about the request of her ghost. She went to find Charlotte.

'You should go and have a lie down. I will stay with Aunty and take care of the guests.'

After her cousin retired, Joan prepared a few platters for the guests then returned to the coffin room.

People walked in to see Mary. They kissed her forehead, caressed her hands, cried, and expressed condolences, then went back to the others and shared their Mary stories.

Joan paced the room. Aunt Mary appeared to her right and walked with her.

'So, you found the things where I told you?'

Joan sighed. 'I found some letters.'

'You must find the ring before they bury me. I am tired. This is unfinished business.'

'What do you want me to do?'

The ghost disappeared for a moment as one of Charlotte's friends came to shake Joan's hand.

'I am so sorry for your loss. She was a great woman.'

As soon as he was gone, Aunt Mary popped up again. 'I cannot remember. There is something in those letters. I searched for the ring after your Uncle Edgar died. I must be buried with my wedding ring.' The ghost trembled and the despair seemed to make her even more see-through for a moment.

Towards midnight, people stopped coming. Joan brought a chair near the coffin and read the letters. Hours later, she was none the wiser on the ring, but her eyes were burning from the candle smoke and the dim light. Just for a moment, she rested her head on her folded arms, hoping to give her eyes a short break. She woke up some time later, startled by a loud bang in the next room. Somewhat dazed, she went into the living room and saw it was morning. She found Charlotte wedged under a cabinet.

'Is everything okay, Charlotte?'

Her cousin banged her head on the cabinet door as she crawled back out. Her face was red, and she blinked away tears.

'I just dropped something.'

'Something like a ring?'

'No, no, nothing important.' She watched Joan with narrowed eyes. 'Didn't you sleep last night?'

'I thought you wanted me here for the wake, so I stayed with Aunty.'

'You didn't need to stay next to the coffin all night. Anyway, we must organise the funeral meal.'

'Sure. What can I do?'

'I have a shopping list for appetisers, drinks and sweets. We need to order catering for the two courses.'

Joan stretched. The few hours of sleep on the chair were not a good idea.

'I'll tell you what we'll do. I will let you look for the… whatever you dropped. I'll go and do the shopping.' Joan turned to leave and then changed her mind. 'But there is one thing you need to do first. Please call the funeral home and ask them to re-do Aunt Mary's makeup.'

'But she looks nice.'

'She looks … promiscuous. And drunk.'

'She was always so happy.'

'Charlotte, not that kind of pink-cheeked happy! And do you know where her dentures are?'

Charlotte nodded. Joan left the house while her cousin was on the phone to the funeral home. She drove into town and, on the way to the supermarket, she drove through McDonalds and ordered a double burger and fries. She ate the fries while driving and dug into the burger on her walk from the car to the supermarket. She heard a chuckle. From the corner of her eye, Joan spotted her aunt again.

'I wish you would stop doing this,' Joan said between bites.

'You cannot get rid of me. Hey, watch out on your left!'

A car entered the carpark at breakneck speed and Joan took a step back at the last second.

'Shit! So close.'

People watched her suspiciously. Joan lowered her voice and glanced to her right. 'Maybe you can talk to me in my mind.'

'You want a ghostly conversation with me inside your own head?' Aunt Mary laughed.

'People are watching me,' Joan said between her teeth.

'And whose fault is that? They cannot see or hear me. You should be quiet.'

'Can you stop following me?'

'Why? So I can't see the junk food you eat?'

'Let me be, Aunt Mary,' she begged.

'You are over fifty and overweight. You must watch what you eat.'

'Enough! I'm hungry.'

'Go and eat sushi. It's healthier. Or a salad. Healthy again.'

Joan took another bite of her burger and glanced to the right just in time to see her aunt pressing her hand on her right hip as if she was trying to hold her hip joint. She had broken her hip many years ago and it had never completely healed.

'I thought there was no pain on the other side,' Joan commented.

'No, there is not. I think this is more like a replica of my alive version. Imagine if you saw me in this old body jumping around like a spring chicken. It wouldn't look like me.'

'Oh. So you are just Aunt Mary. Au naturel.'

A smile cracked on the ghost's face. The delicate body moved elegantly next to Joan, just an inch above the ground.

'I think I may have found something, but I am not sure what it means. In one of the letters, one of Uncle's friends mentions a jeweller, a store called *Art of Gold*. Did you have it fixed?' Joan stopped behind a car and waited for the answer, but she did not stop eating.

Aunt Mary's brow furrowed, and she was again a bit more transparent. 'I think the big stone was loose. We looked for someone in antique jewellery. But it wasn't fixed. Now, since you mentioned it, I didn't see it again.'

Joan finished the burger and wiped her hands. She took out the letter from her back pocket. 'Here it is. This passage.' In the middle of handing the letter to her aunt — to thin air — she stopped, feeling quite foolish.

'So, this store was in Carmello City.'

'Go and find out if Edgar ever contacted them.'

'Well, if the store is still … ' Aunt Mary was gone before Joan finished her sentence.

She took the shopping back to the house, then Googled the store, made a few calls and eventually found a home address for the jeweller. Charlotte stayed away and kept busy in the kitchen.

Joan drove to Carmello City. The drive allowed her time to analyse her actions. She would never have thought it possible to be off on this mission at the request of a ghost, but the ghost of her Aunt Mary seemed as strong in death as she was in life.

Joan arrived at the jeweller's address.

'Is this where he lives?'

Joan nearly jumped out of her skin.

'Jeez! You must find a different way to tell me you are here. You'll give me a heart attack. Anyway, why could you not find his house? I thought you're supposed to see everything from there.'

'You've been reading too many cock and bull stories about ghostly stuff. I can only see and go places I know, or you take me.'

'Hm, all right. Let's do this then. Please try to stay quiet or he will think I'm crazy.'

Joan walked to the house on the narrow path lined by bushes with dark pink flowers. The ghost trailed for a short while. Joan shook her head hoping her gesture would shake her aunt off, then knocked at the door. The man she had spoken to on the phone was a middle-aged skinny man, freshly shaved with light hair that needed a trim. She followed him into the house, where he had to bend his head to avoid hitting the doorframes. The tea and scones were a treat. Joan spent the next two hours in the company of Silvester, son of Jake Donovan the original owner of *Art of Gold*. She talked about her aunt and the lost ring, and her hope to bury her with it. She had an old photo on her phone of the wedding. The ring was a thin golden band with a huge ruby stone and smaller diamonds encrusted around it.

Silvester was sympathetic, but he could not help. He had closed the business after his father died more than a decade ago and he was not aware of any unfinished works. He felt sorry for Joan and her aunt, and he said he would love to come to the house and pay his respects.

Joan dragged herself out of there. The scent of violets wafted from her right. She sighed. Somehow her aunt's ghost would have to find a way out of this world.

'You need to go home, Aunty.'

'I don't have a home.'

'Huh? Then where do you go when you disappear?'

'I am not going anywhere. I am with you all the time.'

'That must be why you are so grumpy. Now you see me every day and you are getting sick of me,' Joan laughed a sad laugh and the ghostly body faded away.

Back at the house, Charlotte fidgeted with the chairs in the coffin room. Aunt Mary lay peacefully in the coffin, not giving away any hint that for most of the day she chased her niece. She had fresh makeup on and her dentures in place.

'Thanks, Charlotte.'

'Anything for her.'

Joan spoke for her cousin to hear. 'Aunty, if you are to be a ghost, will you come to see me or Charlotte?'

Charlotte rolled her eyes. She did not hear Aunt Mary's answer.

'You needed me more than Charlotte. Charlotte would have ended up in a psychiatric hospital before accepting me as a ghost.'

'I don't think her ghost would come to see you, Charlotte,' Joan said. Her cousin blushed. 'And do you know why, Charlotte? Because you are foraging through her things for her wedding ring.'

With flared nostrils, Charlotte stormed out of the room and slammed the door shut.

Joan was left with her dead aunt. 'You know, I reached a dead end. You haven't even shown yourself since we left Silvester. What will happen now? Tomorrow you have your funeral. Are you going to stay behind?'

The ghost did not appear. Joan only heard her aunt's tired voice.

'I don't know. I have never been in such a situation.' Joan was convinced that her aunt was sulking.

While Charlotte did her best to ignore her cousin, they made the last preparations for the following day's funeral. Joan could not sleep, and Aunt Mary remained out of sight. The atmosphere in the house was heavier and more sombre by the hour.

Through the night, more people gathered at the house to view the body before the coffin was closed. Joan stood near the back wall, her eyes red from lack of sleep. She hoped she would be able to say her own goodbyes.

'I am so very tired.' Aunt Mary showed herself on Joan's right.

'I am so sorry, Aunty.' Joan spoke through her teeth.

Aunt Mary whispered, 'Don't be. You did your best.'

'Tomorrow they will come to close the coffin,' Joan said.

*** 

It was the early hours and still dark outside when Silvester Donovan arrived. He gave his condolences to Charlotte.

Next to Joan, the ghost of Aunt Mary started to shake violently.

Silvester went to Joan. 'After you left, I looked through my father's things.'

He took her hand, put the ring in her palm, then closed her fist around it. She blinked fast a few times and swallowed hard. She hugged him quickly and strode to the coffin. She bent over the coffin as if to embrace the dead, kissed Mary's cheek and hid the ring under her aunt's palm.

The ghost disappeared.

Charlotte and the funeral director came in. The man

closed the lid and tightened the screws. The coffin was carried out to the hearse and taken to the chapel for the funeral. The candles were blown out and the candle smoke overcame the scent of violets.

Joan was not needed anymore, and she needed some air.

In front of the house, she watched mesmerised as the early morning fog lifted and revealed the grand spectacle of the hills in the distance. The sunrise was a joy, in cruel contrast with the pain in her soul.

The last gift from her aunt had been a ghost adventure, a treasure hunt to keep her busy, to keep her from dwelling on her pain. She wondered if she would remember anything the next day.

The scent of violets surrounded her.

'I knew you could do it.'

Joan checked to her right. Nothing. This time the voice came from inside her head.

'But you didn't need me, Aunty. You knew all along where the ring was.'

Aunt Mary chuckled. 'You are smart. But maybe you needed me.'

A velvety touch swept Joan's cheek.

'I have to go now, my love. Your uncle is happy to see me.'

Joan held her cheek and hoped to catch the scent of violets. The disappointment was overwhelming. Merciless claws clutched at her heart. Breathing became a burden. Air did not want to move in or out. In the struggle to breathe, she realised she was holding back tears.

Her legs could not hold her anymore. She let herself drop to the ground, hugged her knees to her chest and held herself in a tight embrace while long sobs shook her body. It felt strangely good.

She was ready now to believe it: both the death of her

aunt and the appearance of the ghost.

Because this was her aunt, and she could find a silver lining for any cloud.

## THE END OF SUMMER

I was about to learn how one could lose their whole life as they knew it. I was about to lose ten years. That summer I was just a bit older than ten years old. That summer was almost finished; school was supposed to start soon.

We had just returned from holiday and the servant was arranging our clothes in the wardrobe. The wardrobe was not tall, but she had to use a stool to put some clothes on the top shelf. She had to raise herself on her toes and the skin on her thick thighs stretched — dark from spending time out in the fields. The smell of her sweat was strong in the room.

I could hardly hide my excitement; they would be here any time. I left Lina there, struggling with all the suitcases and went for a wander in the other rooms.

The furniture in the living room had lost its shine under a thick lay of dust. Instantly, I knew my next chore. 'Ala, do you really need to be told everything that needs to be done around the house? Are you blind or something?' That would be the usual way of being asked to dust.

I stepped over the thick Persian carpet and took in the familiar things. The hand-crafted tablecloth was covered in dried petals from the roses left in the crystal vase more than a month ago. The water was long gone, and a brown smudge had dried on the vase's side.

This was my mother's 'good' room; she liked to call it a parlour. Fancy that, in a Romanian communist country, inviting friends over for coffee and tea like her heroines in the English novels, or like the rich people between the wars.

I relished the familiar look of the mismatched family heirlooms on the top shelf in the curio cabinet: a china bone cup and two saucers, two golden teaspoons, antique and ornate, and the silver plate that my great aunt had bought in Paris in 1936. The red geometrical design was faded on the hand-painted Czech coffee and tea set, a present from a big family wedding, and on the bottom shelf I saw the white dinner set with the missing dessert plate.

I was the one who broke the missing plate. It happened when we had visitors once and my duty was to clean the dishes. My mother prided herself on how strict she was with her daughter's education, especially with the learning of the household chores. In her posh ways, my mother liked to change the plates and cutlery for every dish on the menu, and all the plates were brought into the kitchen and piled up on the table for me to wash. There were so many dishes for an eight-year-old. I nipped one plate with my elbow and down it went and into ten pieces. She was behind me in no time. Even the fact that there were guests in the house did not stop her. A quick smack on my bottom burnt like hell, and between her teeth, 'Are you trying to ruin my evening? Break another piece and I will take out the belt.' She had turned around and gone back to the guests with a smile and a reassuring joke. She hated that her set was incomplete, and I had created another drama in the family because that plate would be mentioned for years to come.

I touched the glass panel slightly and my face came closer until I left my breath on the glass. Right there in the back was my most precious little treasure: a tiny bell with a handle crest darkened by time. I knew by now that it had no value; my mother had told me so many times. 'Stop ogling it. It's just a trinket from a fair. Worth nothing!' The little bell looked so delicate and tiny, and my neighbour had said that she recognised the crest. It was an imitation of an old boyar family crest and these bells were gifted at births. This bell was the seed of my daydreams ever since I laid eyes on it. In my dreams I liked to imagine that it was made of silver and related to my birth, that it belonged to my other parents, my other mother. I imagined that out there somewhere there was this sweet and gentle woman, a mother — my real mother — who always hugged me, kissed my cheeks, brushed my hair, read me stories in the evenings, and liked to play with me. I loved horses and I was sure that in my imaginary world, my other mother loved horses too.

I had come to the realisation that I loved the little bell mostly because my mother hated it. I mean, this mother, from the real life. She argued quite often with my father about me. 'She has her nose in those books all day long. She must learn how to keep a house, to cook and clean and do gardening. What will those stories give her in life?' My father disagreed; he wanted me to read. She was also against extra school activities. 'Why do you need choir or guitar lessons? You only do it so that you can stay out late.' Last summer I had spent long hours learning how to iron a man's shirt; no creases were allowed. 'You are so lazy. You refuse to learn, and this is why you cannot do it right. And you are disrespectful.' She did not have the patience to teach me, and the iron felt too heavy. I ironed some shirts several times. I did master it in the end, but after how much shouting? In turn, my father fought for me to keep my books — my excessive reading was never discussed again — and I could learn the guitar. It felt like a victory.

One day I came home from school and found my mother sobbing in her room. My brother told me that she had wanted to throw away my bell, but my father had got mad and said some bad words. Apparently, he had also threatened to cut off her allowance. My tiny bell — the same as me — could create such big problems.

I wanted to slide the heavy glass door of the display case, but my palms would leave marks in the dust. Instead, I just looked at it and felt content that it was still there. When we did the cleaning, I would be able to take it out and feel its warmth, closing my fist around the inscriptions.

'Ala, where are you? Come and help me with the shoes.' Lina's rough voice seemed muffled in the parlour room with its shut curtains, but I followed the order and went to help her.

I loaded pairs of sneakers and sandals on one arm and headed to the dark hall where a tall shelf covered an entire wall. Lina was humming her folk song about a young girl crossing the river to see her lover.

Once finished, I ran out before Lina — now busy in the kitchen — would have the chance to ask me to do something else. I was lost in my daydreams. My mother would come out of the car, tanned, and smiling, probably wearing a fancy summer hat with a ribbon, and she would open her arms. I would bury my face in her neck and smell the soap and cream on her soft skin.

'Ala, you are back!' The shrill call snapped me out of my daydreams. It was my friend Amelia, with a few blond curls coming out from behind her red scarf. 'Come out and play with us.' She carried a huge purse on her arm and on her feet a pair of oversized scuffed high heeled sandals. She came into the small garden.

'I think you'd better wash your face.'

Her blue eyes opened wide, and she covered her mouth with the back of her hand.

'Can you still see it?'

'Yes. There are smudges of lipstick and green eyeshadow.'

She limped next door in a hurry, losing one of her grown-up shoes on the way.

I was immediately surrounded by the children in the courtyard. All the voices were excited to see me, coming closer to touch my hand and asking questions at the same time.

'Are you back now? When are your parents coming home? Did you go fishing with your grandfather? Do you know any new games?'

Gabriella, Amelia's younger sister, grabbed my elbow.

'Do you have to clean? Or can you come out and play?'

She had the same blue eyes as her sister, but her hair was a few shades darker. She pouted and the freckles seemed to come together around her nose. All her face was round: round eyes, nose like a button and a face like a moon. She was the cutest child in our neighbourhood and the youngest one.

'Come on, come and play with us.'

'Where is your house?'

'In your shed.'

'What? Are you crazy? Gabriella, my parents are coming home today. You cannot make your house there.'

'They only need the garage to put the car in. Your father won't mind if we play in the shed.'

'Yeah, but you do not know if my mother is in a bad mood. No, sorry, we cannot play today.'

I did not want my mother to get annoyed with the children playing in the shed, especially the sisters. I had heard her a few times complaining to my father. 'Girls can only bring problems. They are nasty. You need to watch them all the time, and when they grow up you must always watch out for their honour. I don't like them playing with Ala.'

I was in the kitchen washing glasses when I heard the car. Amelia peeked from outside through the curtains with a hard whisper.

'They are here!'

I dropped the glass back in the sink and ran through the corridors, trying to wipe my hands dry on my summer shorts. They were late, but finally here. As soon as I got outside, I saw my brothers skidding their bicycles next to the car. They just let them drop in the dust and ran to my mother who was already out of the car.

She was the same: pretty as a picture, with a summer hat and a ribbon, as I'd imagined her. She was wearing a flowery dress with straps and she looked thrilled to be back. She hugged both my brothers, one in each arm, and started to cover their faces with kisses.

'Oh, my boys, I missed you so much. Let me kiss you.'

And they let her. I was standing there, waiting for my turn, my breath caught in my throat.

'You're here, Missis and Sir. How was your holiday?' Lina asked.

My mother waved her hand in a quick acknowledgement and finally saw me. I moved myself, ready to run into her arms, but her eyes lost their sparkle.

She smiled a frozen smile, and her dreamy eyes looked right through me.

'Hey, Ala. Have you been good?'

She was still holding my brothers close to her bosom. Her golden chain was dangling over my younger brother's head. My arms fell and Lina came closer, putting an arm over my shoulders. Was it to support me or to protect me from making a fool of myself? But I was too stubborn for my own good. I shook her arm off and stepped determinedly towards my mother.

'Now, now, enough hugging and kissing. We have a car to unpack, and we have presents.'

And she turned away.

'Yes, yes!' My brothers were clapping.

I was vaguely aware of the children watching us and Lina's hand squeezing my shoulder. That was what stopped me turning around and running to my room. I swallowed away the tears. If she won't hug me, at least she won't see me crying.

Then I saw my father. He was standing near the car, talking to a man through the window. In the back of the car, a Panama hat like you saw in old photos, half covered a long face. Strands of milky white hair and wide sideburns as white as the hair. His chin rested on both hands, supported by a walking stick. He just sat there motionless with his eyes fixated on me. I blinked away the tears.

My mother went to open the car door and held her arm to help the old man out. My father let himself be hugged by the boys then came to me and hugged me quickly and kissed me on the head. I smiled, delighted.

The old man fumbled for a while with his walking stick. When he straightened his back, I had a glimpse of my father in a much older version. Tall, wide shouldered and a grand manner about the way he carried his body. The old man left my mother standing there without giving her a single look or accepting her offer of help. I could see out of the corner of my eye a twitch on my mother's face; her lips tightened and mine lifted in a cautious smile.

The old man's eyes kept staring at me and I stood there with a sudden feeling of apprehension. He ignored my brothers and shuffled towards me. I felt a pain in my neck trying to look up at him. A crooked smile and his voice instantly wrapped around me with kindness.

'Hello, Ala. I have heard a lot about you.'

His big hand with blotched skin stretched to me and I dared to move mine. He touched my hand with his dried lips, and I felt overwhelmed by his chevalier gesture.

My mother came next to him and, before I knew it, she grabbed me by the ear and lifted me.

'Open your mouth, Ala. Introduce yourself and welcome our guest. This is Uncle Albert.'

The old man placed his hand on my mother's.

'Marcela, this is totally unnecessary.' At the sound of his hoarse whisper my mother let me go.

I could already feel the smack that I would receive after the guest's departure. My ear was burning, and my face felt hot from shame. My father was calling my mother to the car. I sighed when she was gone, and the old man rested his hand on my shoulder.

'I would like Ala to take me inside.' He guided me through the door. He seemed to know the place because he went straight to the parlour.

The next hours passed as in a dream. All of us sat in the dusty living room which was lit up by the late afternoon sun when my mother drew the curtains. Lina was sent out to cut a chicken and prepare the dinner. Uncle Albert was on the sofa and us children were around him where my mother had put us, like in a display. She kept talking about my brothers, how strong and healthy they are, and then apologising for the dust all over the place, then telling us how nice the sand was and how warm the sea was and how many foreigners were holidaying at the Black Sea this summer. Then she told us excitedly about their stop at the old family house to pick up Uncle Albert. He had shown his interest in coming to see the children.

Uncle Albert asked me to bring him a glass of water, and my mother shouted after me not to break something and apologised to him for me being so clumsy. Then, after the suitcases were taken to my parents' rooms and only one big duffle bag was left next to the table, we knew that the moment had arrived. All kind of presents started to come out, like from a Mary Poppins bag: water guns and games for my brothers, a seashell necklace for Lina, handmade tea towels, foreign liquors and cigarettes, a small Turkish coffee pot … and then my present.

'This is for you, Ala.'

I jumped up happily and started to peel the paper from my gift. Emotion surged over me. I reached the plastic photo frame, the size of a copy book, and at first I thought there must be something else underneath. I kept searching in the torn paper and in the back of the frame. I think my face was showing a lot more than I wanted to.

'Isn't it beautiful?' my mother chirped.

I smiled back at her, a wide forced smile, and I lifted my eyebrows in mock surprise.

'Yes, it is. So beautiful. Thank you for the present, mother. This is exactly what I wanted.'

'See, I know you very well.'

Despite my defiance and our polite exchange, she was the one laughing last. Tonight, I was going to bed with a cheap meaningless photo frame in a dirty white with some golden lines. I sat back on the sofa staring at the frame on my lap. How could I imagine even for one second that something — anything — would change?

Lina finished the dinner and father asked her to set the table for the children in the kitchen and for the adults in the parlour. He was trying to send us out of the room to settle the air. I was aware that the old man next to me was keeping me from a belt smacking.

Lina took care of our dinner, showered us, then sent us to say goodnight to our parents and Uncle Albert before she went home.

'But surely either of her brothers is more suited …'

'No.' His voice cut short my mother's words.

'Uncle Albert …' My father stopped when he saw us standing in the door.

After we said our goodnights, we went to the children's room. We were exhausted after the excitement of the day, and we fell asleep as soon as we put our heads down. Later in the night, a sudden noise woke me up. Half asleep, I pushed the blanket away and guided by the moon rays on the carpet, found my way out of the room. In the corridor I could see the light coming from the living room.

'No, I want only Ala.'

I was suddenly wide awake. I leaned on the wall hoping to become invisible.

'I still do not think that is right.'

'I am sure you do not, Marcela, but I don't care what you think. It is the child's right, and that is all what matters.' His voice was raised when he added, 'If you keep insisting, I will stop sending you the money for the house.'

There was silence as I lowered my body to the floor. My back felt the coolness of the wall through my nightgown. I was afraid to breathe.

'I did not know that you would come back for her,' my father said tentatively.

'Before I arrived, I was not sure what I wanted. But I need somebody to live with me. I am old, and I cannot be alone in the house. I know now that Ala is the right one.' He paused and I sensed the humour in his tone. 'I thought that you, Marcela, would be pleased to hear this. I feel that you are not very happy with Ala.'

The silence was complete from my mother.

Uncle Albert added, 'There are servants to keep the house clean and cook, so Ala would only need to keep me company. I still want to read books and newspapers, but my eyes are not the same anymore. And that house is too big and too empty for one person.'

'Well, we could talk …'

'Marcela, I do not wish to discuss this matter further with you. All the previous arrangements were made with Nick. As far as I am concerned, your only role in this affair was to spend the money. Now, I want Ala back.'

Another silence, this time so long that I was afraid they would find me crouched on the hall floor, eavesdropping.

My father spoke again, his voice etched by regret.

'When?'

'Tomorrow, with me,' Uncle Albert added softly. 'Nick, you must know that I value your help. I did not know what to do when both your cousin and aunt lost their lives. But this is the right thing to do.'

My mother changed the subject. 'I need to prepare your bed, Uncle Albert.'

I tiptoed back to my bed. The silence in the house was ringing painfully in my ears. My night became a sleepless time, tossing and turning in bed with their words in my mind.

When the exhaustion finally caught up with me, I fell asleep and welcomed my dream. It was always the same. In my dream, I was surrounded by the smell of freshly baked bread. The woman was there, smiling at me, with her blue eyes and wide mouth, her grey hair in a bun. I always dreamt her so vividly. She was a fat old lady sitting like a ball, round and dropped on a sofa. You could not see where her torso started or ended. Her shoulders sagged, her back bent — just any woman, a stranger sitting on a sofa. The sofa was a French seater, somehow,

I knew that. It was covered with a beige plush, with nice curves on the back rest and hand rests and gilded in gold. The seater looked ugly because of her, and yet there was a tenderness that made me want to join her. In my dream she was not alone. Another silhouette, a thin person, was sitting next to the ball lady: on the edge of the sofa, back straight, head held gracefully, hands resting on her lap. Her face looked delighted. She was beautiful. I could not see her face in my dream, but I knew that.

I shook off the image of the two women in the cold of the night. I wrapped myself in the blanket and warmed myself in its woolly cocoon. I wanted to go back to my dream, but it was too late.

'Ala, are you going to waste all your morning in bed?' The indignation in my mother's voice wiped away the last remnants of my dream. She stood next to my bed and glared, then puffed indignantly and left the room. A few moments later I heard her laughing.

I sat up and hurried through my morning routine. They were all around the breakfast table; when I entered the parlour, my parents and Uncle Albert exchanged looks.

'Boys, since you've finished with breakfast, you should go out and play.' And out they went.

Uncle Albert had my little treasure in his hand, and I stared at it.

'Ala, what would you think if I told you that you could come and live with me?'

He looked me in the eye. My father was holding his breath and my mother was covering her mouth with her tanned fingers. They were all waiting for my answer, but all I wanted to know was how Uncle Albert came to hold my bell.

'I gave you this bell when you were born. It belonged to your great-grandmother. I am happy that you kept it.'

He smiled at me and I smiled back. Was I still dreaming? I sat on the chair next to Uncle Albert and stared at a coffee stain on the starched white tablecloth. I held my palm out and he gently put the bell in my palm. Like so many times in my dreams, I closed my fist around the bell.

'Yes,' I said suddenly.

'Yes what?' It was my mother.

I looked her in the eye.

'Yes, I want to go and live with Uncle Albert.'

All hell broke loose. Everybody was speaking: my father asking me if I was sure, Uncle Albert reassuring me that it would be all right, and Lina hiccupping at the door. My mother started to cry — for effect — and then my father hugged me and kissed the top of my head.

In the next hour, Lina prepared a small suitcase for me, as if I were leaving for a week. She was crying all the time and kept coming to hug me. I was holding my bell; I did not let it go for a second. My palm was already sweaty and slippery around the warm silver.

At noon, a big black car stopped in front of the house. The driver did not get out of the car until Uncle Albert called him. He bowed to Uncle Albert and to me, and for a few seconds his eyes hesitated on my face. My mother showed him where our luggage was. He put it in the car then got back in and waited.

I was just standing there looking at a row of ants finding their way across the path in a neat column. It would rain soon; the ants were restless.

My brothers were still out playing. Apparently, nobody bothered to look for them.

Without a word my father pulled me into his arms. When he let me go, my mother came closer and started to wave her pointing finger at me.

'Now, young lady, never forget where you left from.' Again, the hoarse voice of Uncle Albert stopped her.

'Of course, she will not. This is why she is going back now.' He smiled and grabbed my wrist gently, knowing I was still holding the bell in my hand.

The goodbyes were cut short. We climbed into the back of the big car and Uncle Albert asked the driver to go.

I looked back through the window. I could see my father standing in front of the gate, and he looked somehow stooped, his face ashen. When I could not see him anymore, I turned to Uncle Albert.

'Will I see them again? My brothers and my father?'

'Only if you want to and when you want to.' His voice was soothing.

'And my mother?'

His face darkened and his voice swished the air.

'She is not your mother. She never was.'

'Oh.'

That was the only sound I could utter. And then everything was clear, everything was in its place. Tears of relief poured down my face. She was not my mother, *not my mother.*

## UNDER THE CROSS

The truck cabin had been recently cleaned: no food scraps, nothing in the ashtray, no dust on the dashboard. Despite the cleanliness and the sickly-sweet scent of the car freshener dangling from the rear-view mirror, the stale smell of sweaty upholstery remained, and she found that she didn't mind it as much as she had expected. She preferred to sink back into herself and enjoy the scent — his scent — which lingered on her.

He'd arrived late the previous evening, so late that she'd nearly given up waiting for him. He drove trucks up and down the country for a living, surviving from town to town on whatever food he could find, but he liked homemade stews. After days on the road, her place was a lighthouse in the night — a lighthouse with a good kitchen, in which she liked to cook for him. Last night he hadn't wanted the food; he'd been hungry for something else. The type of man who cleaned his nails regularly and wore a different shirt each day, he'd gone straight to the shower. Afterwards he came to bed, towel wrapped around his waist and still dripping wet; he couldn't wait any longer.

Even though their friendship was a six-month affair, the previous night had only been their second time together in bed. The first time around, he'd been shy, gentle, thoughtful, and cautious. Last night, she'd been pleasantly surprised by the earnestness of his desire.

They had only had a couple of hours of sleep when they began their long drive to the county where his hometown was, his truck loaded with several tonnes of bananas.

'Are you sure your parents will be okay with me staying over?'

She had a few days' leave due and she hadn't wanted to be apart from him after last night, so she'd joined him on the drive to his hometown, but second thoughts nagged at her now.

'It won't be a problem. Just try not to swear in front of them. They're a bit old-fashioned,' he said, eyes briefly turning to her, then back to the road in front of him. 'Besides, they won't be around us for too long. Whenever I'm with someone, they never leave their room.'

'Do you often take lady friends home?'

He rubbed his beard. 'Jealous?'

The headlights of a car coming in the opposite direction highlighted the sharp handsomeness of his features and his long fingered and elegant hands. His broad shoulders were well shaped, and his arms were thick, the strong arms of a man who — at least until recently — had been keeping in shape. Once an engineer in a field where he was no longer needed, now a truck driver. Spending his time on the road had given him a bit of a belly, but he was entrancing, nevertheless. He turned the wheel with the same poise as a conductor waving his baton. Seeing him like this made her realise the sudden depth of her feelings.

By dawn, they'd already covered a third of the distance. He drove silently, focused, while she stared out the window at the craggy mountaintops with her eyes heavy and her mind slow. Through the fog that rose over Caraiman Peak, she could see the Heroes' Cross, a giant metal frame with hundreds of lightbulbs on it. It was always lit at night and during poor weather, always visible from hundreds of kilometres away, and always looking down upon the rest of the world. For a moment, the cross seemed like an omen, but she shook her head to dispel such weird thoughts.

She snapped out of her daze and suddenly became aware of the winding two-lane mountain road, the tight curves, and the steep cliff next to the road covered in a heavy net to hold back rocks and tree roots. Past the other lane was a sheer drop into a deep, forested valley. Her heart tightened with worry but when she looked at him, he clearly wasn't concerned about the mountain or the drop, so she decided to keep her worry to herself.

He drove around a bend too fast, and his truck slid into the other lane; she winced as another truck, coming towards them fast, honked impatiently. He quickly righted the truck, bristling when the other driver sped past with his middle finger up, no doubt shouting obscenities.

He resented any remarks about his driving. His colleagues, all drivers with a lifetime's experience running trucks, took every opportunity to tease him about his useless engineering degree. It irritated him and sometimes made him a dangerously competitive driver.

Unexpectedly, she was on the alert now. She straightened herself and got ready to pay more attention to the road.

He leaned forward; his eyes fixed on trying to overtake the small car in front of them. She couldn't see what was around the sharp bend coming up, and neither could he.

A strange awareness came over her. *Who knows if, who knows what—*

'No!' she whimpered before she even knew she'd said anything. She held both her hands up like a shield … against what?

Startled, he braked with a grunt. The truck slowed down, and he glared at her with an anger she'd never seen in him before.

'Don't. Ever. Do. That. Again.'

Sharply, she pulled back from his anger and turned away from him. When the road was straight again, he overtook a car — slowly, deliberately — and leaned towards her, resting his hand on her knee. Was it meant to be reassuring? She couldn't tell.

From behind, a small green Mercedes was trying to make its way ahead of them. It was a stubborn and noisy little gnat of a car, tailing them closely and trying to push them against the side of the mountain so the driver could get his way.

'You stay where you are, you idiot,' he muttered, both hands returning to the wheel to hold it steady.

The well-known feeling was back: *the irrational fear* that came with a wave of nausea that washed over her. Her hands trembled uncontrollably, so violently that she had to steady herself by clutching her fingers together. She looked out of the window, trying to find anything that could distract her from the edge of panic. It did not help. She broke into a cold sweat. Through the taste of bile rising in her throat, she just couldn't get enough air. She was aware of the sweat under her armpits, on her face and neck. Before she could do anything about that, the image was there. With the eyes of her mind, she could see a white cross; her eyes darted towards where the cross should be, up on the peak, but it was out of their sight. It did not matter; she could just *feel* the cross bearing down on her.

She closed her eyes. It was completely pointless because adding to the feeling and the vision, the third sign engulfed her: *the smell*. Her nostrils filled with the scent of burnt candles, as if she were in a church with hundreds of praying breaths and clouds of candle smoke hanging above their heads.

Her thoughts stuttered. *What? What is happening to me?*

He was confused about her erratic gestures and moaning.

She leaned forward, both hands on the dashboard now, trying to focus.

*What am I supposed to do?* She wanted to run. Anything to stop the haze of agony and panic descending upon her. She searched her thoughts and, through the swirling mess in her head, one word kept surfacing, fighting out from the mix of scents and fear: *stop, stop, stop.*

The terror, the image, and the smell. Yes, this happened before, but this time she knew better.

She had to follow her instinct and listen to it, obey the urge.

'Stop the truck!' she hollered.

And this time he did as he was told. He pulled the heavy truck over and parked it in a rest area next to the mountain.

'Are you okay? What's going on?' he asked her. She couldn't answer.

The driver of the green Mercedes, now free to rush ahead, held his horn down as he sped past. She could hear his voice, as angry as the shrill siren sound of his horn, and she saw him for the briefest of seconds: a dark-skinned man wearing a red cap. Another impatient driver in a powerful machine on a treacherous road. The man next to her pushed a bottle of water into her hands, which she pushed away violently.

The truck stayed in park for a few minutes while she tried to just keep breathing. He watched her, afraid to do anything else, afraid it could make this worse.

Then, as quickly as everything had started, it was over.

The smell cleared and the terror was gone, leaving behind a sudden calm. Her head fell back on the headrest, and she closed her eyes. She found she couldn't turn to look him in the eye.

She couldn't tell him about the last time, when she woke up in the middle of the night with the same blinding terror, when she saw crosses on graves alongside a road, and when the same smell surrounded her. And later, when the release from the panic had come, she'd just collapsed into an exhausted sleep. And later still, when she'd learned that one of her neighbours had had an accident in his house and bled to death, to be found two days later.

Now, she inhaled, exhaled, and found it easier with each passing moment. She could finally look at him. Worry brought extra years to his face and his eyes. At least he was alive. This time, this one, was alive.

She whispered, 'Are *you* okay?'

'Of course, I'm okay! What was all that about?' He sounded annoyed.

She returned his puzzled look and lied. 'I'm not sure.'

She paused and searched for the feelings inside her, but all was silent and peaceful. She almost smiled. 'We can go now.'

His hand rested on her shoulder, warm and reassuring. 'I *am* sorry I shouted at you.'

She lightly brushed his hand away. 'No, it's okay.'

'Are you sure?'

'Yes, we can go now.'

He didn't seem entirely convinced, but he still had a job to do so he slowly returned to the road after one last searching look her way.

Less than a kilometre down the road, they saw it.

Strange, the details that stayed with her: his deep frown, the brakes squealing as he reduced his speed to get a better look, both of them looking wordlessly at the bodies spread over the tarmac, something red — a red cap — in the dry grass by the road, a basket and apples strewn everywhere.

Of the two cars that had collided, one of them had flipped and the other one — the green Mercedes — was crumpled to half its length. Later, she would remember the stillness of the air, the truck moving in slow motion, the sunshine weaving through the treetops in the ravine.

Next to her, her man leaned out of the window. 'What happened?'

The man directing the traffic pointed at the flipped car. 'Came from the opposite direction, in the wrong lane.' Then he pointed to the Mercedes. 'Just in the wrong place at the wrong time. Nothing he could have done about it.'

They didn't speak the rest of the way. When he stopped the truck in the warehouse parking lot, he killed the engine, exhaled noisily, and lowered his forehead to the wheel. Finally, he lifted his head, and collected the shipment documents from the glove compartment. Before he got out, he looked her in the eye.

'I am not sure if I should be afraid of you or be thankful.'

# DO NOT DISTURB

T here was something about the sign hanging on the door that she did not like. It was the hotel standard — in font, size, colour — with the hotel emblem and the twisted red rope. Had it been perched the same way for the past two days? She could detect a funny odour coming from the room behind.

All day she went up and down this corridor, going about her chores and cleaning the rooms, but this time she stood in front of the door longer than before. She quickly checked left and right; her supervisor would not like her poking her nose into the guests' rooms when the sign was clear: *Do Not Disturb*.

She rapped lightly with her knuckles. Nothing. Maybe she had not been loud enough. She increased the taps. Still nothing. Finally, two loud knocks. 'Housekeeping!'

Her hand searched with trepidation for the master key. She swiped the card and pushed the door open. The rotting smell hit her physically. She covered her mouth and nose. When she stepped in, it struck her how staged the room was. There were two bottles of champagne placed on the left and right of the mirror and two stools placed either side. The bodies on the bed were aligned with the bottles, while their arms — her left and his right — were outstretched with the hands parallel to the stools. The sun ray that sneaked through the curtains glittered bloodily on her red-stoned ring. Their clothes were neatly folded on the stools, with the shoes placed underneath. She had to admit, everything was neat and tidy. The bodies were covered with a blanket, and they were holding hands in the middle. Small blisters covered their faces and arms. She finally noticed a discrepancy: his eyes were closed and hers slightly open, as if she were taking a sneak peek through her eyelids.

The maid turned and ran out. In the corridor, she closed the door behind her and gasped for air, only then realising that she had been holding her breath. Her handset receiver hung on her trolley bar. As if in a trance, she picked it up and pushed the button for her supervisor.

'Miss? It's floor three. Gina.'

'Where the hell have you been? I've been calling you for half an hour.'

'Miss!' Gina interrupted. 'I was only away from my trolley for few minutes. Miss! You'd better come up here.'

She waited with her back against the wall, thinking about how she would have to see the bodies again.

Her supervisor — tall and plumpish, red in the face, fuming eyes and moving surprisingly fast — stormed out of the elevator.

'You! I don't have time for disrespectful staff!'

A door opened and a man in a bathrobe looked out, confused. The supervisor slowed down and smiled at him reassuringly. The man returned to his room and Gina swiped her key card again, pushed the door open and gestured her supervisor inside. Gina followed her and, when she heard her supervisor wheezing and gagging, she thoroughly enjoyed watching and barely hid her smile.

Then, once again, Gina took in the arrangement and the tidiness of the room. She would have to close the woman's eyes properly as soon as she had a chance, for her work of art to be complete.

It was already much better than her last one. She felt proud.

## NOTHING HAPPENED AT SCHOOL TODAY

I asked for black coffee, no sugar,' the man says in French. His annoyance is accompanied by a cup clattering down onto a saucer in clear protest.

She is a traveller of the world, enjoying the trip of a lifetime in Greece and immersed in all her interests: history, architecture, gods and myth, and temples. Of all the places in the world she could hear this rough voice, it is here on a cruise on the Aegean. The voice instantly begins to unspool memories, and the past comes back in images, snatches of conversation, the music she grew up with, and the smell of dusty courtyards. Slowly, she is taken away from the lower deck of the cruise ship to a place that, until now, has belonged to her childhood, to a place and a moment that has deliberately remained lost to her, as vague as Piraeus Harbour and Athens fading into the hazy September morning.

There are muttered apologies, then another clink of china. She hears his voice, even more aggravated as the waiter has clearly got it wrong again. She can relate to this man's frustration. She understands the importance of a good cup of coffee, especially as she sits there sipping her first of the day — perfect, as far as she's concerned — because she didn't have time to get one before the tour bus came to the hotel to pick her group up before the sun even began to rise. But the rich, dark scent of her Greek coffee in the blue and white demitasse is no longer enough to cover the smells, the horrible smells evoked by that unravelling memory.

She remembers a girl just a few years her senior, ripped from her family in the early hours of a Monday. The girl's mother cried and held onto her daughter's hand for as long as she could.

They never saw or heard from the girl again, of course, and the theory was that she'd died in some prison hospital after being tortured for information on who had helped her get an abortion.

They'd been illegal in communist Romania — abortions — and severely punished. Any girl or woman who had such an intervention was labelled a traitor to her country and was declaimed as a whore. One shuddered to imagine the sort of treatment a girl with that sort of stain on her name would have received in prison.

And what does that voice, that man, have to do with this awful memory?

She turns her head, gaze slowly panning over the faces of every stranger on deck. Near the small bar stands a group of seniors, men and women, and there he is: a stooped man arguing with the bartender and gesturing dangerously with a cup. He is so old that the joke about death looking for him at home instantly comes to her mind; she suspects he's on this cruise just to avoid that meeting. His hair is snow white and so thin that his pink scalp shines through it.

Over this image, she superimposes the image of the same man, but from decades ago. His hair was already white then, but it was a thick mane, tamed only when he ran his large, callused hands through it. As rumours went, people said he watched his wife die, and his hair started going white a few weeks after she finally passed away. He was tall and unbent when she knew him them, with a wide face and a chiselled chin, and a large nose that suited his intelligent face. He was her maths teacher in lower secondary school, and he drank — after his wife. He was grudgingly respected by everyone, tolerated by most, liked by only a few, and absolutely hated by Mrs Popescu. It was her who relayed to the Department of State Security everything he did and said, especially on *that* day at school when they found *the thing*. So, they took him away on the same Monday as that girl, never to be heard from again.

What she remembers is a wide courtyard, with the bare ground hardened from thousands of feet trampling on it. Since Easter, the old chestnuts had been full of rowdy collared doves. Their cooing echoed through the yard when children were in classes; it was a sign that summer was fast approaching, and excitement for the long holiday was mounting. During the breaks, their beady eyes would follow the kids' impromptu games of football or leapfrog. The girls would jump rope and talk about boys, and high above them the collared doves would cock their heads and listen in.

She remembers the school buildings as if she's seen

43

them yesterday: stark concrete masses of brutalist architecture, the yard enclosed with limewashed walls that were blackened with soot and mould. What at first sight seemed to be random square concrete slabs spread across the bare ground were in fact pathways leading to different buildings. During the rainy season, these squares became islands in the flooded yard, all the better for children to skip from one to the next, laughing. At the back of the yard, nearly out of sight, was a block of toilets. It was so old, it could have been heritage listed when Carmen was a child — or better yet, it should have been torn down. The boys' section was at the back, and the girls' section at the front, and the area was always clear of any play because the smell was so bad, especially when the weather was warm — as it was that day.

The air was permeated by high-pitched screams of delight, and the raucous joy of children playing football. She was the only one of the girls who ever played football with the boys. In the middle of the game, she stopped and raised her pinkie.

'Wait! Carmen needs to go pee. We can take a break.' The team captain, a tall chubby boy, lifted his chin towards her, as a go signal.

She remembers running towards the toilet block and taking deep breaths about ten steps away from the entrance, then holding her breath against the smell. If she moved fast enough, she could get in and out without having to breathe again. She stepped inside carefully and peeked into each stall to find the cleanest one. The first one was a no-no. The second one had a puddle of urine on the floor. She was running out of time. But when she looked into the third stall, it was even worse. Carmen couldn't help the gasp. One of the other girls must have just started her monthlies, but come on … on the floor? Or was that what she thought it was?

Intrigued, she forgot about the smell and stepped into

the stall. One of her shoes was in the blood now, and she cringed. She stretched over the toilet as best as she could without going further, until she could look down into it. The seat was missing, and the bowl was brown from all the human dirt. And right in there … she couldn't stand it anymore. She turned around and, as soon as she was out of the stall, she vomited her breakfast right under the cracked sink, the one with the tap that hadn't had running water in years.

Funny how she remembers that grimy sink now, of all the little details that could have stuck with her all this time. She remembers running out of there near-blind with terror and bumping into the eighth-grade maths teacher. She craned her neck to stare up at him, into his wide nostrils with the long white hairs. His eyes were red, and he hiccupped. 'What on earth are you doing?' he bellowed.

'I … There …'

'Speak, child!'

'Please …' She pointed back into the toilet block, tears of fright rolling down her face. 'I think there is something in the toilet.'

His frown didn't change one bit as he strode into the toilets. He returned very quickly, his bloated face dark.

'Go to the teachers' room and tell Mrs Popescu that I need her to come here.' Carmen turned to run and heard him say through gritted teeth, 'And don't say anything to anybody about this.'

Carmen doesn't remember the mad dash to the teachers' room, but she did return with the history teacher. The maths teacher asked Carmen to wait outside and signalled Mrs Popescu to follow him. She heard his grave voice, then a squeal.

She knew then that Mrs Popescu had seen it too. Carmen glanced around to make sure no one else noticed this was going on, then followed them into the toilets. She stood there half hidden by the door frame. Both teachers were in front of the stall.

'This is insane,' Mrs Popescu said, and she seemed to choke. 'How? What happened?' Before he could reply, she continued, 'Oh, the smell here is horrible.' She took out a handkerchief and covered her nose.

The maths teacher stepped into the stall for another quick look, then backed out.

'Mrs Popescu, I do hope you do not expect *me* to tell you what happened.'

She straightened herself up with a huff. 'You're drunk.'

'At least it helps with this smell,' he said grimly. 'I cannot tell if it's full term or not. Can you?'

'No, I cannot. It is … I'm not sure.'

Carmen thought about going closer to the stall but hesitated. She flinched whenever she thought she had touched anything in the toilet, shrinking away from the walls and the stalls and the sink and into herself.

'Well, we need to call the police,' said the maths teacher.

'And the party committee. This will ruin our plan and credentials with the party for ever. The communist party takes great pride in the proper education of our young pioneers and young communists, and that includes their moral education.'

'I don't give a shit about what the party thinks,' the man retorted, shoving his shaking hands into his pockets.

'You shouldn't say that. If anybody hears you, you'll be taken to a labour camp next. We need to make sure that the children don't find out about this.'

'Did you notice any girl with … *problems*? Can we guess who it was?'

'This is such an inconvenience,' Mrs Popescu said, almost to herself. 'A very unfortunate event and we need to be very careful about how we deal with it.'

The maths teacher turned to face his colleague fully, his expression stormy and unforgiving. 'You're delusional. Somewhere out there is a girl that just gave birth, or had an abortion, in this *shit* hole, and you are worried about *the inconvenience*?'

Then he saw Carmen standing there. Their eyes locked: Carmen's filled with tears, the man's filled with sadness and despair.

And then, he was gone. Gone from the school, gone from the town, gone from everyone's lives, and everyone who wondered what happened to him knew without a doubt that he'd been taken by State Security. Only Carmen and Mrs Popescu knew why.

But he is standing here now, on a cruise ship in the infinitely blue Greek waters, so he survived. Whatever ordeals he was put through by the communists, he survived. His voice sounds older, but not weaker, and the harsh tone and sarcasm are the same as she remembers. Listening to him berate the bartender and tell him how his coffee should be made brings back memories of being taught formulae and equations. She only remembers them because of this obstinate man.

It's him alright. Probably over ninety years old by now, but with the same wit and sharp tongue that never suffered fools.

Done teaching the bartender his job, the man turns and catches her smiling at him — or at the memory of him — and their eyes lock for a moment, like they did so long ago. His eyes are still the icy blue she remembers. Maybe more frosted over by age, but she recognises him. From him comes a flicker of recognition as well. He frowns. His left eyebrow goes up. Then, finally, his mouth opens in a wide smile that shows perfect dentures. The look they share now is understanding, commiseration, regrets for lost time and lost lives.

He walks to her table.

'Tu eşti, Carmen?' he says in Romanian. *Is that you, Carmen?*

She nods, lost for words.

He puts a hand on her shoulder as if to make sure she's really there, and he's really there with her. A tear finds its way down a cheek covered in liver spots and burst capillaries.

'Mă bucur mult să te văd. Arăţi bine.' *I am so glad to see you. You look well.*

Finally, she finds her voice.

'Şi eu mă bucur, domnule Ursu. Mă bucur să ştiu că aţi scăpat cu viaţă.' *I'm also glad, Mr Ursu. I'm so glad to know you lived.*

They share a few more words, some pleasantries that are meaningless in comparison to the stark joy she feels at seeing him again, and then he leaves the same way he came. He walks back to his group and to the life he has now.

Though Carmen is now left with the dark, heavy memory that has been revived by the sound of his voice, she feels lighter, somehow.

## THE SLURRY PIT

In the heavy rain, the road seemed to go nowhere — like her life. With the back of her hand, Sara wiped the foggy windscreen and tried to peep through. The wall of water was just another shield that she could hide behind. Still unable to see, she rolled down the windows as she drove slowly along. The rain was coming in, and she enjoyed the wet smell of leaves and mossy bark. On the top of the hill, the rain had stopped; the woodland was engulfed by a cold fog, the kind that hung on clothes in droplets. She saw something on the ground in front of her car. She pulled over and went to have a look.

He lay on his back, legs and arms sprawled wide as if

he had dropped to make angels. He was an ox of a man, broad boned, with a bloated face covered by a thick beard; this must be why, at first, she had thought the mass on the tarmac was an animal hit by a car. His eyes were closed and sweat gleamed on his forehead. She grabbed his hand and shook it. The hand was soft and clammy.

'Hey, mister! Are you okay?'

She pressed her palms into his huge belly. His eyes flew open. Mad, dark pupils fixated on her anxious face.

'I was …' His hoarse words were reduced to a mutter. Sara leaned closer with her ear next to his mouth.

'What is it?'

He gasped for air. 'I was tired. I wanted out of there. All those memories.'

'Out of where?' She lifted her head and struggled to look through the fog. Both sides of the road were lined with tall, straight trees, so dense that there was no whiff of the wind she knew was ravaging in a storm just down the slope. There was no car in view. Her breath was visible in the cold air when she whispered, 'How did you get here?'

His murky eyes penetrated her spirit. Everything stopped there, and time became relative. His thoughts tapped into her brain, but there was a kindness that let her feel all right. He took her hand and walked with her. Somewhere away, between old days and things, between spaces. She saw room after room, streets and corridors, houses, faces, cities, rivers, mountains.

She pulled her hand away abruptly. 'Who are you? What do you want from me?' she asked. Or did she? Maybe she just thought it.

He did not talk, but they were both inside her brain. There were a staggering number of corridors walled up with drawers: some of them transparent, some sophisticated white wood, others coloured in flaky paint of green, blue, or red. Some were inky and cobwebbed, with mud dripping from them; those ones smelled bad, and the smelly muck made her pull back.

She reached for a stack of coloured drawers. She saw herself on the ground, beaten up, on her knees, wailing in pain with a broken mouth; she saw herself crying on the toilet seat in a single-room apartment on the ninth floor, hiding from her children while they slept; she saw her husband, drunk, throwing an empty bottle at her; she saw herself on that January morning when she went to see her father in the hospital, only to find that the bed was not only empty, but had already been made. She saw the clean, white sheet stretched across it and she saw herself as she was then, leaning against the wall for support while tears choked her. She knew there was a scream in her throat, held back only by her willpower.

She hung onto this aching echo until her vision was obscured by the bearded man. She had tears on her face.

'Step aside. I want to stay here,' she said. 'There is something unfinished.'

He held his hand out. 'Let us keep going.'

His hand was an open viaduct with warm water as he led her to another drawer. The comfort of his hand took the edge off the vicious winter in that memory when they had travelled for eight hours on icy roads in minus twenty-five to take her father to his chosen burial place.

The man moved her towards a cobwebbed drawer.

'Not yet. I don't want that one,' she said, like a petulant child.

She went for one of the white drawers — of course she would — and feverishly pulled it out. That year they were walking on sunshine. High school year eleven, officially seniors. The freshmen looked up to them and the teachers were friendlier. The days when students were accepted as young adults. She was a top student and always busy. That year she was arranging a play for graduation.

She saw the science teacher, in his early forties, long

face, big nose, suit and tie. There was a smell. She looked down at her shoes. Had she stepped in something? He had considered himself one of the cool teachers, ready to lead evolved discussions in which the students' ideas and opinions were taken seriously.

She saw herself in a light blue shirt and dark blue pinafore, with a few acacia flowers in her pocket. She was asked to present a lesson, but she didn't have time to prepare. The teacher seemed ready to accept her excuse, but her big mouth got the best of her. She pompously declared that sciences were complicated, that she did not like the subject, and she had no intention of pursuing a career in that field. She saw her peers roaring at her bold words. She was such a smart-arse. This time the teacher failed to take the joke; instead, the popular girl received a mark below passing.

She pulled the next drawer open: blue coloured. She saw herself feeling confused when, in the following weeks, the teacher asked her to present in every class, then grilled her until she failed. She saw the battle between her popularity and his power. It seemed everything came at a price, including speaking your mind.

She saw herself defeated. She was flunking science. There was a meeting in the head teacher's office. The consensus was that Sara should memorise and be tested from an entire chapter. The science teacher would tutor her after class.

She saw herself studying in his office for a week. Again, that manure smell came from nowhere.

Sara tried to move on, but the bearded man grabbed the elbow of her mind and steered it back. He pushed her through the cobwebs. She held her breath against the sludge.

She saw the teacher casually placing his arm on her shoulder, pulling her closer to him. His hand was stroking her back, lower and lower. The sewage smell was in her nostrils. With her face burning, she pushed his hand away. His arm was back on her waist, fingers digging into her flesh. Her skin was crawling under the filthy muck. She tried to get out.

She saw the teacher pushing her against the shelf, his hands cupping her breasts. The shiver, the recoil. She was sinking in slurry. What was happening? Her arms were fighting his hands; her eyes were focused on a speck of wool on his shoulder. Her jaws clamped against the horrid smell. She cried, 'No, No, No!'. How many times? There was a knock on the door. The teacher froze. Sara grabbed her school bag and ran out.

Sara saw herself taking the tests and passing; she saw herself avoiding the teacher's gaze; she cursed her big mouth, cursed her popularity, and hated science even more. She saw herself fighting against revulsion with every simple gesture of a friendly hand on her shoulder.

The bearded man watched Sara closely as she finally raised her head and looked the teacher in the eye. The acacia flowers were overpowering the smelly muck.

In a cove tucked below the stormy woodland, the ocean was bringing in foamy waves which washed away the slurry pit. The horizon was lit by the sunrise.

## THE FIVE-DAY PLAN

The fog and grime that covered the town was slowly seeping into my soul, each day a little bit more. The communist austerity hit me so much harder here, where I was not supported by my father as I was back home. But this was my path because I'd failed my university entrance exams, but still wanted freedom. For an eighteen-year-old, that meant accepting a state-allocated job at a spinning factory about eighty kilometres from home. I took it as my punishment. Life slowed down.

My accommodation was reduced to an uncomfortably small room that I shared with two other girls. The room was at the back of the garden of a big house and had once been used as a summer kitchen. The only amenity was a sink that we had to share and use for cooking, washing, and bathing. No point getting into details about how we managed that; it's enough to say that we became quite inventive. The toilet was an outhouse.

I attempted to get an audience with the party secretary of the factory, to ask for what they called a 'redistribution of accommodation', hoping I could live in one of the Romanian-government-factory-owned apartments. As soon as I filed my request, I knew I did not have a case and I would not be a priority; apartments were first distributed to higher positions, and then to families with children. As bribery was, in one way or another, expected in these kinds of dealings, I realised that some cigarettes and palinka might help my case. I just did not know how much would be enough. If only I could get the audience so I could properly discuss my case, but four months later I was still waiting.

Of course, if you wanted to get something — anything — you had to have the right connections. Just the previous month I'd finally dared to approach my foreman at the factory with a different request.

'Could I get some more shifts?' I was desperate to work weekend and night shifts, which were paid better.

He stared at me blankly for a minute, almost surprised by my nerve. 'I'm not sure.'

'But I really need them. I'm on minimum wage and I can barely pay my rent.'

'Everybody needs them,' the nasty man told me with a shrug.

I only had to find the right thing to say. 'I'm going home for the weekend. We have a wonderful palinka there.'

He appeared to ignore my words, but still said, 'Come and see me when you get back.'

It was the first time I had tried the power of the bribery by myself. Two weeks later, lighter a few litres of palinka — plus some oil, sugar and flour, which were on ration cards but my father had free access to — I began to pull more shifts, and then a weekend and a couple of nights.

It was rather warm for the end of January. The snow had begun melting immediately after the new year, and the roads were covered with a blanket of dirty slush. The potholes, both on the pavement and the road, were real winter traps. You could easily step into an ankle-deep puddle and twist an ankle. During the night, freezing temperatures covered the streets with a layer of ice, and the town looked slightly polished.

I spent the night in an apartment, somewhere in the industrial district, with a bunch of people that I had never seen before in my life. In the living room, twenty-three of us were crammed on sofas, armchairs, and the floor. It did not bother us. This was a video night, when one of the black-market guys played movies he'd smuggled into the country from the free West, all night for a modest fee. Going to these video nights was a regular occurrence for me, maybe once a month. The films fuelled my imagination. Among others, we watched a movie that took place in West Germany. I kept thinking about the hero who ran through the pouring rain to his car, then chased the villain in hot pursuit. I made the comment that there were no potholes or puddles on those streets, but one of the guys said that they only used especially nice streets for filming. And the cars. There were so many, coming from all directions and honking. There was so much life and noise. The streets were never that lively and crowded in Romania. Not with the fuel ration.

I wondered what it would be like to go to work in my own car instead of taking the bus or trudging through melted snow. I wondered what it would be like to live somewhere like Germany, where they had clean and well-lit streets, and well-stocked stores, and real American brand jeans — not the rough imitation Romanian denim that we had. To make our jeans look worn we would rub them in the bathtub with a brick.

The daydreams didn't leave my side. No wonder these video nights were illegal. Happy people lived in Germany, meeting in cafes and talking on the streets; while in Romania, Ceauşescu and the Communist Party decided for us how we were going to live our lives: impoverished financially and spiritually, struggling each day, not just to survive but to embrace the brainwashing. They were keeping us busy with the Party Congress and the five-year plans carefully crafted for every town, school and factory. We were supposed to work on achieving the plans, put on happy faces, and find unknown meanings in our indoctrination. Of one thing I was sure: after all the cold we endured during communism, we could never be threatened by the flames of hell.

The video nights were a way to defy the regime, but I also enjoyed them for another reason: the merchandise. The guy smuggled stuff from the Federal Republic of Germany: music cassettes, coffee, cigarettes, chocolate, soap and deodorant. And because I did not know when my next chance would be, I got carried away and spent the last of my money on presents, even though the birthdays I was buying for were months away. My father loved a good cigarette, a change from the filtered Snagov that smelled like grass. Only God — and Ceauşescu — knew where all the local tobacco went. All autumn, there were fields of good-smelling, golden tobacco, but Romanians were left with damp and foul-smelling cigarettes made from stalks and grass and wood chips. Cigarettes that had to be lit ten times. So, everybody liked a good foreign cigarette. Additionally, foreign cigarettes, chocolate, and real coffee brought in from abroad made for the best bribes.

For my mother, I bought Fa soap. I was in awe just from inhaling its perfume through the wrapping. Even these days I put soaps between clothes to get them perfumed with the fragrance of the forbidden and inaccessible item. My mother would scold me for buying this German soap, this foreign triviality that lathered up into sweet-smelling, clean foam. Wasn't her homemade soap good enough anymore? Was her daughter too good for it? Was she above it all now? Secretly, my mother loved the soap. It was a luxury that I wanted her to have after years of watching her make soap from each winter's collected fat, oil and gristle left over from cooking. At the end of a long and arduous day spent boiling lard and rancid oil with caustic soda, we had hand-cut soap with the lumpy texture of oatmeal and the lingering smell of fat. Growing up, both me and my sister washed our lustrous, thick, long hair with this soap, then rinsed it with water and vinegar: our parents' and grandparents' shampoo and conditioner methods handed down through the generations.

In the early morning, after a night spent watching movies, the smuggler let me sleep on the floor for a few hours so that I would not have to go home through the dark, the snow and the icy streets. With the Kent ten-pack carton and four bars of Fa safely tucked into my bag, I walked for half an hour to a cafeteria that I knew about. The brown slushy snow got through my boots to my feet and made my toes slide in my wet socks. Inside, the cafeteria was barely warmer than it was outside, and I blew warm breath into my cupped hands as I walked to the corner where the buffet was set up. Excitedly, I picked up a tray and joined the queue.

I didn't look at any of the food on display, because I couldn't afford it, but I helped myself to a huge bowl of bean soup, a couple of chillies and a few slices of bread.

The label proclaimed it as 'fasting bean soup', and that was exactly what I was there for. Not for the fasting — God help me — but for the price; there was no meat in the soup, which made it the cheapest meal in town, and the portion was generous. The soup was hot, thickened with flour that had been fried with oil, paprika and tarragon. The herbs didn't quite overpower the underlying taste of burnt flour, but I had not eaten in almost a day. I had spent almost all my money on presents my mother could turn her nose up at, and now I couldn't even afford the bus ticket to my hometown to get some food and bring it back to my cramped quarters. Besides, I was too proud to call my family and ask for help, especially since this was not the first time I had done something this foolish. I would just have to bear it for the next five days until I got paid, and spend my spare time reading and drinking plenty of tea.

The soup was filling, and the chilli warmed me right up, fortified me for the trip to the spinning factory. It was a feeling of fulfillment that I would always remember. I saved the bread, folded it into a napkin and put it into my bag. That night, I would burn one spoon of sugar in the bottom of a pot and add water to boil. And I would have that 'tea' with the bread. Maybe I still had some beans and lentils in the little cupboard in the shared room, and a couple of onions, and some potatoes. With some Vegeta stock powder, some oil, and some austerity-born creativity, I could make my own soups. Somehow, I'd make that last until I got paid.

Back out on the wet street, the morning air was hazy with dark clouds and fumes from all the factories. There was a commotion of some sort as I left the cafeteria, with people running in the opposite direction.

'What is it?' I asked a young girl who'd stopped to wrap her scarf around her head.

Happily, the girl said, 'They brought cheese and sour

cream to the grocery store.'

I smiled and continued in the direction of the factory. My shift would start at two o'clock, so there was no time to join a dairy queue that already stretched to the end of the street — not that I could afford it anyway. My priority was getting to work and dealing with my wet feet. I had sneakers and overalls in my locker at the factory, so at least I would be dry.

As I passed the bus stop near the factory, a bus pulled away. It was overcrowded as usual, with the doors open and people riding on the steps. The stop was now empty. On the bench I saw a crumpled and abandoned pack of cigarettes. I looked around, but there was no one to claim it. I approached the bench slowly and sat down, covering the packet with my coat, then my palm, then sliding the pack into my pocket. Glancing down, I saw it was unfiltered Carpați, and the packet was still dry. I squeezed it, hoping it hadn't been abandoned because it was empty. Luck was on my side. There were still a few cigarettes in it. I took my time rolling one between my fingers to soften the herbs, then let it rest for a while between my lips. For a few moments, I enjoyed the cold air I inhaled through the unlit tobacco. I looked in my pocket for a lighter.

Lead clouds hovered over the town, and soon big snowflakes started to dance down. My lighter flared in the dark day and the flame flickered. Holding the cigarette between my thumb and forefinger, I lit it with a short puff, quickly followed by a second, lingering drag. My head swam as I inhaled. I hadn't smoked in days.

As I stood up from the bench and smoked the cigarette, with my belly full but my feet still wet, I was surrounded by clouds of smoke. Snow slowly filled the folds of my coat. The day, and the week ahead of me, already looked better. As I took another drag of the cigarette, my right hand was absentmindedly counting the coins in my pocket.

## BLOUSE OF A DACIAN SORCERESS

After two weeks Anca was ready to believe in the supernatural. The thing that had been following her on this trip did not waste time with light obstacles. A soft mist started to lift off the ground as soon as Anca unfastened the straps of her rucksack. She challenged it and carried on removing the shoulder straps. A cloud of fear eclipsed her reasoning when, in retaliation, her legs were encircled by icy cold air. She stated her surrender out loud.

'Okay, I've got it. Not here.'

She buckled the straps again and kept walking between the haystacks.

With ease, *the instinct* prevailed.

For many years, every summer without fail, Anca had spent a month trekking in the mountains. This time, though, her trip in the Apuseni mountains had an alternative purpose: to collect material for her Master of Ethnology thesis. As she knew she would, she had found plenty of material in the isolated villages. Each morning she planned her route, which village she would visit next, but during the day — pushed by unknown forces — she would be diverted towards a different village.

At first, she dismissed the signals: fallen branches across the paths, rustling noises in the forest, sudden downpours, sunken tracks, roads blocked by flocks of sheep. She would spend most of the day going around the stumbling blocks or trying to remove them. Until it became too tedious, and she slowly started to sense which way to go to stay free of obstacles. Little by little, she allowed herself to be steered. She called the weirdly forceful guidance *the instinct*. It just crept up on her, but in the end she accepted it. She put it down to the innocence of the wilderness; she could let go and let nature lead her along.

This last trick seemed quite original. It was the first time *the instinct* had used fog.

'Spooky!' she whispered and laughed at the fog. She kept walking and moments later, when she glanced back, the fog had vanished. The haystacks resembled sleeping giants in the warm light of the summer sun.

'Might as well find a bed for a few nights,' she muttered.

In a short while she found a tiny hamlet with less than twenty houses. The houses on both sides of the country road were dominated by a fountain with a shadoof and a deep trough for watering animals. The village had stopped in its tracks one hundred years ago, with no electricity, phone line, gas or running water.

A sun-bleached sign read 'Farmhouse — Bed and Meals'. The house, clean and cool, had the smell of the wood fire smoke impregnated in its walls. The old couple agreed to rent her a room and provide meals. She feasted on a spinach mash with garlic and cream, and balls of cheese melted in hot polenta. The high bed, which was covered with warm bedding, looked like a better option than camping out in the cold night. For all the cold and tiredness, the weird and the spooky, Anca felt as if she fitted in to this place.

The next morning, after a cup of cow's milk — freshly milked and still warm — she took her camera, notebook and phone and went out to look for the village museum. The search did not take long. A few houses away she found a gate which had 'Museum' engraved across it in elaborate calligraphy. The house had white walls and a beautiful garden with short rose bushes. She climbed the few stairs to the front porch. The warm air of the summer's day followed her into the musky low-ceilinged room. Two tiny windows covered with minuscule lace curtains were the only source of light. One wall was covered with pottery and handmade towels, a wooden bench held a massive stack of loomed blankets, and the wool carpet still carried a vivid red and black in its pattern of flowers and geometrical figures. Popular folklore clothing was also displayed: Romanian traditional blouses, called *ie*, and the *fota*, a skirt like an apron which wrapped around the body. All the handmade clothing was stitched with representations drawn from nature. Anca had seen hundreds of similar objects in the past two weeks.

She heard a cough behind her. She turned to see an elderly man smiling at her.

'Welcome to our village. I am the caretaker.'

'Thank you. Your museum is beautiful. How old are these things?'

'The oldest ones belonged to our great-great-grandparents.'

'Is there a cellar in this house?' Anca asked. 'I study ethnology, and I'm travelling to do research about folklore and traditions. Cellars are dry and cool, and usually the storage place for all kinds of objects. Those are the interesting ones.' She gave him a wide smile.

'You know your way around our museums.'

He walked to the oven built in the wall, took a petrol lamp, and lit its lamp wick. Holding the lamp in front of him, he went through a narrow door. She followed him.

'Over the years we have had a few students coming to see us. They catalogued our objects and took pictures of our women weaving carpets at the loom. They even interviewed our oldest Babas. But nobody has ever asked me about the cellar. I have not come down here in a long time.' He caught his breath at the bottom and lifted the lamp towards the dark chamber.

'It is a bit dusty, but you can look around. Just be careful how you touch the objects.'

The ceiling, slightly curved, was low enough for her to touch. The chamber was crammed with barrels, old furniture, baskets, and parts of looms. Every available surface was crowded with anything from pottery to tools. In a corner Anca saw the dowry coffers, their panels painted with flowers and birds.

'You are staying at the farmhouse, yes?' the old man asked, well informed.

She nodded. 'Thank you so much for letting me do this.'

'Well, I hope you find what you need for your studies. If you find something interesting, we can restore it for the museum. I will return this afternoon. If you finish before then, please bring the lamp up and tun out the light.'

He handed her the lamp and left her there.

In the bowels of the old house, she dug the dowry

coffers out from under layers of wispy cobwebs. She blew the dust from a lid and started to take out clothes. Great-great-grandparents meant three generations, more than a hundred and fifty years ago. They looked older than anything she had seen so far. The design of the embroideries looked more complicated and denser. Some items felt dry and ready to fall apart, others needed repair. Various scents wafted from the coffer: grass, wood, lavender, but curiously no dust. It should feel wrong to enjoy touching other people's clothes, especially dead people's, but Anca relished it. Spooky.

One *ie* became her favourite item in an instant. From a fine linen already stiff with age, it had finely woven black frames around the neck and wrists, and large sleeves embroidered with intricate patterns.

She spread it across her knees and squinted in the bad light to make out some of the symbols in the design: the pine, wheat, hook, column, the cross, the wheel. There was a tree with branches, flowers and leaves on each sleeve. She loved the warmth and happiness irradiated by this work of art. The full embroidery doubled the thickness of the garment; it felt heavy on her lap.

As if reunited with an old friend, she held it in her fists and buried her face in the crusty yet delicate fabric. She inhaled its scent: goldenrods.

She lost track of time trying to break up the motifs. When her eyes got tired, she religiously folded it, placed it back in the coffer and carefully closed the lid.

She carried the lamp back up to the museum and killed the wick. Outside, the sunlight temporarily blinded her. She knew she would be back when she realised she had forgotten to take photos.

At the farmhouse, the host delighted her with mushroom stew and a yoghurt like she had never tasted before.

That night she had a strange dream.

*In a Dacian temple, a wounded warrior and three Dacian priestesses sat around a fire. The priestesses wore the ie with heavy black embroidery. One of them stirred a cauldron over the fire, her lips moving in quiet words. They spread the potion over the warrior's wounds. The cauldron was a silver vessel decorated with the Dacian flag, weapons and bearded faces of Dacians. Anca touched it, and it did not burn her hand. With her fingers she felt something etched below the rim, and she recognised the symbols: the pine tree, the wheat ear, the shepherds hook, and the column.*

Then the dream became noisy.

*There were battle cries, the clash of weapons, and the neighing of horses. A woman dressed in leather armour carried the Dacian flag. The sleeves of her ie with black embroidery fluttered in the air.*

*'Protect the priestess,' one Dacian warrior cried. The priestess lifted the Dacian flag and the wind passed through the hollow tube shrilly. 'The Legacy of a people stands in us!'*

*The Dacians, with a cry of war, followed the priestess in attack.*

*The Romans tried to escape.*

Anca woke up still hearing the vicious battle and the scimitars slashing into limbs. She rendered it a privilege to see her ancestors so vividly in her dream. She knew that she had had the privilege because of the *ie* with the black embroidery. This time she was one step ahead of the instinct and she returned to the museum.

The caretaker did not look surprised to see her again.

'Do you know the source of the black *ie*?' she asked directly.

His smile disappeared. 'Come with me. You need to speak to Baba Derina.'

'Who is Baba Derina?'

'She is more than one hundred years old. Even she

cannot tell you from what depths of time she comes.'

At the end of the village, the old man pointed to a beautifully carved gate, then went on his way. Anca's intuition told her she had finally arrived at her destination and found a wonderful secret — even if she did not know what it was yet.

The gate was barely holding on to its hinges, and the yard was covered in high grass. At the back, the dwelling had walls made of a mix of clay and straw, and a thatched roof. Everything appeared to be on its last legs. The heavy grape vines spread onto the roof, almost as if they were trying to pull the roof to the ground. Anca stopped a few steps from the open door and called out.

'Hello? Is anybody home?'

She heard movement and, in the shade of the vine, spotted a small person sitting on a narrow bench. The Baba's face was like wrinkled parchment. Her head, shoulders and back were covered with a black shawl, despite the hot summer. She wore a white *ie* and a long *fota* folded over layers of skirts. Her feet were hidden under the mass of fabric. Baba Derina held a sliver of bark between her gums.

'Aye,' she said, her dark brown eyes watching Anca with intensity.

Anca whispered the traditional, most respectful greeting for old women.

'I kiss your hand.'

The old woman cawed; it was how she laughed.

'You have felt the thread.'

'The thread?'

The old woman slowly slid off the bench, spat the sliver of wood onto the grass and gestured for Anca to follow. She barely came up to Anca's shoulder.

The massive metal rings clinked against the wood and the hinges creaked when she pushed the heavy door. She limped and dragged herself inside.

Anca squinted in the badly lit room. On the clay floor, there were a few ragged carpets of indefinite colours, caked in layers of mud carried in over many years. There was a strong herbal smell. Anca lifted her eyes in search of the source, barely avoiding hitting her forehead against the dried plants hanging off the ceiling beans. Long stemmed plants, small bunches of flowers, clumps of twigs and tree bark, and tobacco leaves hung from lengths of rope.

There was a table with a top of thick dark wood, its surface covered in cuts and scratches. It was packed with jars and vials, potions and powders, a mortar and pestle, a clay pitcher and a few candles. Above the table was pinned an old religious Christian Orthodox calendar. Curious, Anca leaned over. The paper had Sundays marked in red, as well as Easter and all other major celebrations, all the Saints' name days and the fasting periods. A real agenda for the churchgoer. Anca heard a wheezy breath behind her and turned quickly, ashamed to have displayed such impolite curiosity, but the old woman smiled with her toothless mouth and her eyes showed understanding.

With her bony hands, Baba Derina grabbed Anca's wrists. She felt the skin on her arms prickle with a pleasant sensation and a flow of energy trickled into her veins. Baba let go when her touch started to burn.

'You are one of our blood,' Baba said. She pointed to a piece of furniture. 'Sit.'

Weak on her knees, Anca bundled herself onto the small stool.

'You've had the dreams, yes? How many?'

Anca lifted one finger.

'Aye,' Baba said again. 'Four more will come, and you must learn all you can from them.' She sipped water from the clay pitcher. 'They will come again if you summon them.' She watched Anca as if searching for something in her face and repeated her words. 'You are one of our blood. I don't know how it is possible. As priestesses we were not allowed to know men. But one of us must have done it.' She cawed again with her throaty laugh. 'She was your many times great-grandmother all the way back to Deceneu, the high Priest of Dacian King Burebista, around 44 BC.'

From under the table, Baba pulled out a shoe box and put it on the table. The Adidas logo on the box was a sharp reminder of the present.

Baba Derina took a baby chick out of the box. The chick, barely a few weeks old, had started to change, the white down on its wings turning dark grey. It had a hooked beak, maybe an eagle chick. Baba handed the chick to Anca. When she took it in her cupped palms, she noticed one of the wings was hanging awkwardly. It was broken.

'You want to make it better, yes? Use the warmth in your hand and your breath to heal it.'

The words overpowered Anca's sadness and chiselled into her mind. She had a strange feeling that her thoughts did not belong to her anymore. The sizes and proportions of the room changed, and she found herself inside a sphere of solitude, deafeningly silent, where she was oblivious of place and time. Her body fell limp and she was disturbingly aware of the vigour in her blood. As though through thick glass, she heard Baba's words.

'Enclose it in your palms.'

Anca's hands went soft around the shivering chick's body, leaving the broken wing visible.

The bird's heartbeat throbbed all the way to Anca's ringing ears. The skin across her cheeks stretched until it felt taut and tender. As the edges of her face smoothed out, the pointy bits sharpened: her chin, nose and cheekbones became more prominent. The heat coming from underneath her skin threatened to turn her inside out.

She heard the muffled voice again.

'Blow your heat onto the wing.'

Anca lifted the precious load to her lips and sent a gentle blow. The chick cried with a high chirp. When Anca opened the palms, the wing had settled back in its place as if it had never been broken. The chick looked at her with one beady eye, full of appreciation.

When Anca's body lost its heat, the sphere of solitude shattered. Her ears flooded with noises from the day outside. They were ten times more powerful than usual: the wind in the trees up on the mountain, birds chirping, a cow mooing a few houses away, the water in the fountain.

Slightly weary, Anca shuddered. Her body tried to wake up and her mind fought to understand. Baba took the healed chick and put it back into the box.

As if helping Anca to return, Baba spoke.

'The gift awakened inside you. The *ie* reminded you who you are because only one of our blood can feel the embroidery.'

Anca gathered her strength and asked. 'The cauldron in my dream. What is it for?'

'Aye. It is a vessel for ceremonial offerings. The potions prepared in it are powerful. You must keep the knowledge from your dreams and, when the time comes, you will know what needs to be done and how to use your knowledge and your power. Each time will be easier.'

'It's *the instinct*.'

She smiled again with her hollow mouth. 'Aye. You could call it that. I know it as power of a goddess and witchcraft of a priestess.'

'How old are you?' Anca whispered as if afraid of the answer.

'Aye. I have forgotten. But I was one of them, the priestesses.'

'How is that possible?'

'The blouse. If you wear it all the time, it adds years to

your life. I got tired of life wearing mine and I put it away. The blouse called you here.'

'Do *I* need the blouse?'

'All you need is in your blood. You have just revealed that with the bird.'

'But why is the blouse—?'

'It's the column of life, the infinite of rebirth, stitched with thread of ancient bison hair, and skin of the cave dragon simmered for days with herbs and gold dust from these mountains. It took a long time to create the thread and to embroider the blouses.' She took another sip of water. 'We made seven of them. And when we wore them, we could only die in war and of spear.'

Anca left the ancient woman and her ancient house, exhausted and in a daze. She slept all day and through the night.

She had the second dream.

*They were in a mountain pass and one of the priestesses led a group of riders through a narrow way. The Dacians knew it was a trap. The Romans attacked from the peaks and circled them. The warriors fought until their last breath. A spear thrown from afar hit the priestess in the throat. She broke it off, leaving the tip inside, and her eyes smiled to the death. She held on to the horse's mane. The horse carried her to a woodland and then to a clearing where two priestesses were waiting. They received her body, washed her, put earth into her fists, and covered her with flowers to prepare her for her final trip.*

Anca woke up in tears. She hurried to Baba's house to share the dream.

The curator waited at the gate.

'Yesterday, after you left, Baba asked me to bring her the *ie* and she burnt it. She gave me this for you. She knew you would return and wanted me to wait for you.' He sighed away the tears. 'Baba Derina died overnight.'

He handed her a heavy package wrapped in plain brown paper and tied with thin rope. Anca went back to her room. Shaking, she opened the package. She smiled as her fingers brushed the symbols below the rim. It was not a dream anymore.

The cauldron now belonged to the last of the Dacian witches. She just needed to find another blouse.

# THE 1979 SUGAR BEET HARVEST

During communism, school years were defined by the farming practice. That day was about harvesting sugar beet. The sun gleamed on the autumn dew; the fog hovering over the ground hid our boots. We breathed steam out of our mouths, ready to warm up with the work ahead. The field of dark green leaves as far as our eyes could see lowered in the wind with a deep hush.

We teamed up. Our competition was who could finish their rows first. The first line pulled the beets out and threw them in a pile, the second line chopped the leaves off the roots.

To chop the roots, we created our own routine:

positioned around the pile to easily reach the beets, we picked up a root with the left hand, then dropped the knife in a ready move where the leaves came out of the root. The leaves were left on the ground and the roots were thrown into the truck. Our bodies were in concord, dancing like the old clocks' ballerinas with lifted arms and twisted heads. After only a few hours, our dance was properly memorised.

I had a brilliant knife — extra big and sharpened by my brother. From an old bag, he had also handstitched a sheath with a nice clasp. The four of us stood around the knee-high pile of beets left behind by our classmates; the sugar beets in this pile were silenced, and no wind rustled their leaves. We became machines: pick up, hold, lift the knife, lower the knife, swish, chop, throw.

I lifted my nice-looking knife. Next to me, Carmen was singing *By the rivers of Babylon, there we sat down*. For a moment there, my mind drifted. I started bringing the knife down. Its blade was honey coloured from the sun. I liked Boney M, and Carmen's baritone voice sounded warm in the air that was permeated with the sweet smell of the chopped roots. My elbow, for the nth time that day, moved back, then front, up and ready to complete the same motion as a coupling rod on the wheel of a train.

Near my beet, on my thumb, I saw an ant crawling. A big red ant. Should I blow it away? No, I didn't want to break up the routine. My heart was flooded with a warm intuition, in contrast to my ice-cold feet. The beet in my hand was muddy, my thumb was captive on the beet, and the ant was moored on my thumb. Was the knife on the way to chop the ant? The knife moved down.

And then I screamed 'My finger!' Was it in my head or out loud?

The knife reached my finger. The knife slid through it. I felt hot even with the chill wind on my back. My face

went pale joined by immediate nausea. I dropped the beet
and the knife as if they were burning.

And I stood there, holding my hands out like a blind
man finding his way, with my fingers spread. All but one.

With the nice-looking knife that my brother had
sharpened for me, I had chopped my finger off. Carmen
was singing *Yeah, we wept, when we remembered Zion.*

## THE BABY THAT SHOULD NOT BE
## TALKED ABOUT

Joe's voice was thin. 'I am not going to be the father of your love child.' He thrust her body against the railing then grabbed her legs and gave her a shove over the parapet, his sweaty palms sliding on her stockings. She was a big white wing on her way down. The last thing he saw was the surprise in her eyes and her red-rouged lips in a cute pout. Then the grey morning took her away.

There had been a storm a night before, and the white dress was a spot on the surface of the mad swirling waters. She could not swim. In her struggle to stay afloat, the veil twisted and covered her face. It should have been the veil of her innocence. He watched the body being taken by the churning water under the bridge. It twirled one last time then went under.

He went back into the wedding reception on his own, playing the happy groom. At four o'clock in the morning most of their guests were at an elevated level of happiness. This was the reason why earlier it had been easy to take her outside unnoticed.

'Can we go out for a walk?' he'd asked her. 'I want to be with you.'

She touched her stomach and smiled coyly. 'I think the baby would love to get out of here for a while. It is a bit too hot.' Sweat dripped down her cheek and he smiled away his wish to smack her.

He took her hand and walked her past the tables then right over the middle of the dance floor. The dancers were getting crazy with their swing moves while 'In the Mood' blasted from the speakers. Still holding hands, they stopped for a few minutes and danced with her aunt and uncle. His bride hugged them and shouted, 'Thank you for introducing me to this wonderful man who made an honest woman of me!'

With growing impatience, he clutched her hand and pulled her from the crowd.

'You are a bit rough with me. You need to remember that I am a pregnant woman.' She walked fast, with small paces.

'Like I could forget,' he muttered to himself.

The hotel's terrace narrowed as they reached a romantic, old bridge. Early morning in the mountains was cold, but it helped to calm the wedding agitation.

\*\*\*

The wedding party had lost its charm two hours ago, when Joe was in the toilet, of all places. He had been in one of the stalls, his presence unknown to his best men who stormed in, all drunk and merry. He overheard words that carved painfully.

'She tricked him with the baby. It's not his,' the first one said. Joe heard a zipper and a strong jet of urine hitting the basin.

Seated on the toilet, his heart sank. He had to stay quiet. He heard heels clicking on the marble floor, another zipper, and a second voice.

'Such a fool! He is a good catch for her. Graduated among the top five, so all major hospitals and a couple of private clinics would want him on their pay.'

The third one laughed. He seemed to only be there for the joy ride, or his zipper was silent. 'Maybe if he wasn't so busy studying, he would have seen what she does.'

'Now he is a married man and that's it,' the first one stated. Joe could hear the water running and the paper towels being dragged out of the dispenser.

'He gave a name to that … that … love child,' the third one reiterated.

Their laughs faded away as they left the bathroom.

*** 

Joe could see them now: all three of them, his university friends and colleagues, as they sat at their table. They laughed noisily when they saw him coming. He waved, feigning joy.

He seized a bottle of beer at the bar and drank half of it in one swig, then asked for a carafe of draught beer. In a swift move he drained the crushed pills into the carafe, then headed to his mates' table. He stopped next to them, his face contorted in humiliation, but they were too drunk and happy to notice.

The first one asked him, 'Where is your bride, you happily married man?'

'I took her to the room. She wanted to change her dress.' He showed them the carafe. 'Give me your glasses, my best men. You need to drink for the groom.' He filled their glasses, then raised his own bottle. 'As we used to. Bottoms up!'

They all drained their glasses and smacked their lips at the cold fizzy beer. The second one raised his hand. 'By the way, do you know why Harry couldn't come to your wedding?'

'Not really. I think I received a card from him, but I didn't get around to reading it.'

The third one chortled. 'Poor sod! He had to get married urgently.'

The drunk friends guffawed at the gossip.

Suddenly Joe's stomach was replaced by a black hole. He swayed for a moment before his legs gave way. He sat on an empty chair. Barely breathing, he whispered, 'Why?'

'A bird got her claws into him.' The first friend coughed and wiped his forehead before finishing. 'She got pregnant, and Harry has no idea that the baby is not his.'

# THE GOOD, THE BAD AND THE UGG

Coming to Australia was, at most, a dream: one of my first dreams as a young girl, when I was trying to resist the communist regime. We were not allowed to speak, so having these dreams was a rebellious way of saying 'I detest communism'. I imagined that one day I would defect. I would run away from that life of ration cards, of soap and deodorant purchased on the black market, of restricted news. A life cooped up in the cage of the Communist Party.

I came up with two options: Canada and Australia. Australia was my favourite option because I wanted to go as far away as possible. As a girl I had heard a lot about ships coming from Australia to our Black Sea ports. Early on I became committed to English classes at school, both because of a natural talent for foreign languages and because my instinct was telling me that one day I would need English.

But how was I going to travel to the Black Sea? How could I find an Australian ship to hide on? How much food and water would I need to survive hidden for a few days? How far would the ship need to go before I came out of my hiding place without risking being sent back?

Then life started to take my dreams apart.

I got married and had my daughter in 1989, in the same month and year as the revolution came to Romania, and Ceausescu was executed. My dream was not a fight-for-my-life necessity anymore. My father had real hopes for Romania to return to the rich society that it once had been between the two wars. It did not happen — not then and not ever since — and he died before any remote glimpse of past times returning.

Then, my son and my divorce came very close to each other, and I found myself a single mother of two in a patriarchal society. My drive and intellect were an impediment. This is how I spent the next twelve years, not hating the Communists anymore but hating the inherited mentality.

My life in Romania was lived with a sense of unrest. But even when, at long last, my dream did come true, I was not prepared for the challenge it turned out to be.

I met my friend on an online chat forum. As if ET was ready to come home, it was my first contact with an alien: an Australian. My exotic online friend who was to become my husband.

Less than two years later, I landed in Australia. It had only taken me twenty-eight years.

I came — or in fact *we* came — to Australia, ready to take the world by its enigmatic horns. I was positively happy to be with my man and ready to show my children what opportunity means.

One month into the adventure, they hated me and hated Australia.

It was July, rainy, cold and windy, after coming from a summer in Bucharest where we'd spent the last week before departure by the pool. The Australian rented weatherboard house was chilly and half empty. There were no carpets, and the second-hand mismatched furniture smelled of the sweat and unwashed feet of previous owners. We called it 'the shack' and we meant it.

On a weekly basis my children and I would 'accidentally' find ourselves together on the living room sofa, where we would talk about memories of friends and family. Talk and cry until early mornings.

In time, the weekly crying meetings became monthly, then even less frequent. From the beginning, though, I was afraid to ask them if they were happy. I knew this wasn't home, and I did not want to hear their answer.

The months went by and it was not easy to see the looks of disappointment on my children's faces. My heart went out to them. I was feeling the same, but I could not let them see that. I had to be strong, for their sake. I started to grow knots in my soul. I was afraid for my children, that if they didn't like the new country and their school, they would rebel and start using drugs. The result of living with this constant panic was that my children distanced themselves from me.

They were children, just children, who were supposed to feel secure and have simple, happy lives. But it seems they had to grow up before even having the chance to be children. At least we were going through it together.

As it turned out, my children are as free-spirited as I am. They have a low tolerance for ignorance, stupidity, unfairness, injustice, bribery and communist mentality.

After their first visit back to Romania, they stopped hating me for bringing them to a new continent. They went through a rainbow of sensations and emotions learning about their new country and new life. I believe they each found their own way to enjoy the new opportunities and started to build their own nest to call home.

Nowadays, we do sometimes sit and talk for hours, but there are no more tears.

So, how was our life?

Well, one morning, in the first month we were in Perth, my son came to breakfast with a face clipped by awkwardness. Hesitantly, he asked, 'Are there monkeys in Australia?'

We laughed at him, thinking he may have been dreaming, but he was convinced that every morning he could hear a monkey under his window. We continued to laugh, but my husband had the answer.

And so it was that, with good humour, we met the kookaburra, which we all still jokingly call 'the Australian monkey'.

Then there was the time we ran out of milk. It was late in the evening and we needed milk for breakfast.

My husband, happy to oblige, told me, 'There is a deli down the road. We can go there.' I was interested to know where this place was so I would know where I could walk to next time. In Romania, 'down the road' means what it says: literally, down the road. You walk for five or ten minutes to the closest intersection, and there you are: down the road.

Well, we got in the car to go to this deli, and we drove into a beautiful Australian night — one of those evenings when you want to drive into the sunset with opened windows surrounded by the smell of wet leaves. The aromas of the Australian plants overpowered the night air. No matter how enjoyable, fifteen minutes later we were still driving. Did we take the scenic route? Was my husband planning a romantic drive? On the dark and empty streets, another five minutes passed before I looked at my husband and enquired, 'Where is this place? I thought you said it was just down the road?'

'Oh, it is,' he said, and drove for a few more minutes. Finally, he parked in front of a lit-up deli, where the shop assistant was watching an empty store and three deserted fuel pumps.

My husband excitedly said, 'Well, this is it.'

'This is down the road to you? Down the road was ten streets back. Down the road was five lights back. This not flaming *down the road*!'

We went in and got the milk, and I sulked all the way back. All of a sudden, the Australian night was not so lyrical.

And so, with irritation, I met the deli-down-the-road.

We argued about 'down the road' endlessly. Or, better to say, *I* argued. I was in a foreign country, and already in my first month I was fighting against it, as if I had never left home. I had no idea what was happening. If I could not even understand my husband, how was I supposed to shield my children from all the bad things in the world?

Suffice to say, I learned not to ask 'how far' it was to some place or another, but rather 'how long does it take'. If I heard 'down the road' again, I would go ballistic. Do I need to mention that I never had the chance to take an easy walk down the road to that deli?

Or, how about the time — also in my first few months in Perth — when my husband offered to take me to a shopping centre.

'What shopping centre?' I asked excitedly.

'It's something like the malls in Bucharest. Maybe a bit smaller, but still, lots of shops, supermarkets and eating places.'

In Romania, every time we go out of the house — to the shops, the doctor, for a coffee, to a pub, even to visit friends — we dress up. We wear our good-going-out clothes and shoes. So, on the day of the visit to the shopping centre, I got ready. I showered, put make-up on and got dressed in a tailor-made woollen skirt, hand-knitted jumper, and handmade high leather boots. I remember them, even now, a beautiful dark blue colour. I also remember something else: it was the last time I wore those boots. I insisted on my husband changing his Perth Glory soccer t-shirt for a proper shirt and knitted jumper. I was a very good wife, but if Australian life had been a school subject, I would have failed miserably.

We arrived at Belmont Forum. Me: impressed by the immense car park and the huge building with its unknown number of entries and exits. My husband: happy about my delighted face. We entered the Forum, hand in hand. Fifteen steps into the building I stopped in the middle of a round hall, surrounded by the smell of freshly made coffee. My mouth was agape. And not because of the coffee. As I stood there, embarrassment rose into my face. In my fancy winter clothes, I looked like an idiot and felt like an idiot. I was also sweating like an idiot.

People were walking up and down, going about their business and totally at ease, dressed in shorts, t-shirts, jogging trousers or summer dresses. And on their feet … wait, *wait*, this was what surprised me most … Ugg boots or thongs, flip-flops. Shorts with Ugg boots, shorts with thongs; dresses with Ugg boots, dresses with thongs; jeans with Ugg boots, jeans with thongs. Occasionally there was a light jacket or flimsy jumper and a scarf around a neck. At first, I thought this place was unique, but over the years I learned this was actually a popular Australian costume.

And so, with shame, I met the thongs and Ugg boots.

I hated thongs and Ugg boots for a long time, turned my nose up and avoided them like cholera. It took me years to reconcile myself to the feeling of inappropriateness, bad taste, and fashion faux pas. I hated that in Australia you needed to put a notice at the door of the pub asking for proper attire and stating that no thongs were allowed. I was critical about it, but I was the new kid on the block, and I was not here to change anything. I just had to accept that thongs and Uggs would be part of my life whether I liked it or not.

Now I go shopping in shorts and Ugg boots or thongs.

I went back to Romania; it was seven years after I moved to Perth. I had to go to the store to get some missing ingredients for a dish I was cooking. I went to the supermarket down the road — which really was a five-minute walk — in shorts, a t-shirt, and thongs. My cousin frowned. 'Are you going out like this?'

Me, being innocent and not giving a rat's behind, replied, 'Yeah. Who the hell knows me here?'

Well, as I was about to find out, that was exactly the point. They did not know me, and me showing up at the store dressed like a beggar made the guard take a cautious step and place himself in front of the entrance, as if trying to stop me from getting in.

I frowned my malicious frown with my left eyebrow lifted high and my lips shut tight. Something in my eyes must have deterred him because he backed up and let me go through.

In my home country I felt purged and rejected, and in Australia I was unadapted. I wondered so many times, what I have done to our lives? If our move to Australia was not going to work, I would have destroyed my children's lives so very easily. A fear of uncertainty and disconnection dominated my life for many years. I was a guest in both countries.

Then, how about the time when I experienced my first Australian summer?

Well, it was January. I was working from home while our three children were at school and my husband was at work. I did not have a car, so I decided to walk to the shopping centre — a good one hour walk there and back, I estimated. Just perfect to stretch my legs.

It was a gorgeous day, with a cloudless blue sky which almost seemed surreal. No change of nuances of blue and no spot of clouds. I was ready to go out at about eleven.

I started my walk and, thirty minutes later, when I realised I was lost, my blue morning walk turned into a nightmare. I could not find any familiar buildings, and the streets all looked the same. I tried to find my way back and changed direction a few times, only to end up in an industrial area. The heat was above my head and all around me. I was thirsty and felt the sun burning my face and arms. My feet were heavier with every step. I knocked at doors which remained closed. I started to panic, overwhelmed by a feeling of sheer loneliness. One cannot understand loneliness unless they walk for hours in the midday sun on streets that seemed unlived in. When I finally saw somebody, I wondered if she was a ghost coming out from the waves of heat floating on the street. She was real and she told me the right way. It came as no surprise to hear it was in the opposite direction.

I dragged myself back to the house where I arrived after three hours in the sun without a hat or sunscreen, exhausted and dehydrated. I sprawled on the sofa, with heatstroke finally taking ownership of my mind, after crashing my body. My mind could barely process what had just happened and my eyes blindly stared at the curtains which I dutifully pulled over the windows. I just wanted to stay away, shaded, hidden, and protected from the nasty sun.

Of course, I'd been in the sun before, I'd been sunburnt, I'd even had bad heatstroke in my life before. But this… this was an Australian experience. This time my encounter did not anger me, but instead it frightened me, and something else, humiliated me.

My people had sandwiches for dinner and I spent the night awake and filled with doubts. Australia was another planet. I was not home and maybe I did not belong here.

And so, with humility, I met the Australian summer.

In my second year in Australia I got a job outside the house. I worked in a medical clinic and every lunchtime we would lock the front door and sit in the reception to have lunch together. For months, I listened to them talking and tried to participate in the conversations. I was only guessing the meaning of their words. I could not understand the slang, and I could not separate the words which seemed stuck together, some of them five in a row.

Feeling as if I was underwater, I experienced a complete deafness to the meaning of the words. I sometimes cut off completely. I only pretended to listen until I shut down and out. It was exhausting to pretend that I understood what they were saying, and only rarely did I risk answering back. I was always missing the point and making a fool of myself. It took me a while to admit I was struggling and let them know they needed to speak slowly for me. They had a good laugh and finally understood my weird behaviour.

And so, with anxiety, I feared the Australian slang.

When my son first called me 'mate' I felt insulted. 'I am not your *mate*!' In Romanian there is no such word between men and women, let alone between mothers and sons. There are pals, friends, colleagues, drinking buddies, but not mates. But, it took me a few years to get it.

I could not finish without mentioning the 'How are you today?' When I was first asked this question by a shop assistant, I thought she must know me from somewhere, then I thought she was nosy. The girl, in her Aussie laid-back way, was just greeting me politely, even though I did not think she expected an answer. She hadn't made eye contact, which was for the best as she could not see the puzzlement on my face.

I was so worried about all the misunderstandings, so anxious about all the things I could not get used to. I could only see this 'How are you today?' as an empty platitude. Why would somebody bother asking me how I was if they were not even looking at me?

It took me long years to embrace the question and to reply, 'I am good, thank you'. Even more years to ask, 'And how are you?'

Ten years of my life I lived as if I was in a slow-motion movie, placing one foot in front of the other cautiously, allowing all my dreams and plans to become hazy. Before I could think about my prospects here — building a life, building a house — before anything else, I had to learn to live the Australian way. First, I had to deal with anger, fear, shame, bewilderment, uprooting. I was new and an immigrant, exiled from my family and friends, from my customs and food. As the years went by, I felt like a moth trapped by the light. There was no way back, and it seemed the way ahead was harder than I had thought.

Oh, I don't know why I am writing about all these things. Australia has more immigrants than Australians, so to speak. There are so many people who have had their thong moments, listened to a laughing kookaburra, or fought the heat of a day. But here I am, fifteen years later, and Australia still amazes me. Every day I still learn something new, every day I still see something new. Over the past year, with Covid, I have started to feel that I finally belong. The Covid times made me reassess the meaning of words like 'mate' and questions of 'How are you?'. The events of the past year have made me realise where my place is. I've been in the right place to witness the united front put on by Australians, people believing and accepting that only together can we get out of this shit.

I am now happy to be Romanian-Australian. I will

never stop being Romanian and I will never be fully Australian, and that's okay. I think I have finally succeeded in removing the constant guilt that I deserted my country, and that in Australia I should do more to be part of it. It does not matter too much, because in Australia being an immigrant is essentially another kind of citizenship. And I am okay with that, too.

It has only taken me fifteen years.

Once, somebody told me and my children, 'Go back where you came from, you stupid immigrants. Nobody wants you here.'

But you know what? I do belong in the place where I can ask 'How are you today?' and I belong in the place where mates are. Clearly that person did not know the real meaning of these words, and maybe they were the ones who didn't belong.

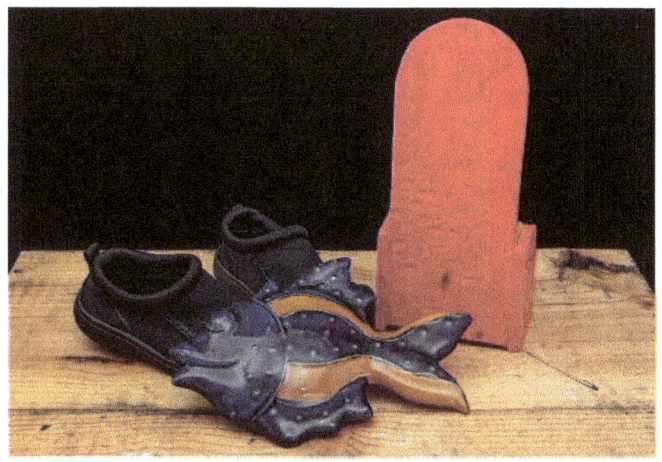

# GILBERT THE GIANT GOLDFISH

You never believe some things unless they happen to you. People tell you about dreams, premonitions and weird stuff that happens to them. You say, 'Nah, it's just a way for them to get attention.' Then, the weird-something happens to you. Can you tell anybody about it? Of course you can. Only you already know they will never believe you.

Charly was nearly seven years old when he disappeared. He vanished one foggy May morning. Did he vanish? Did he get lost? On the coast of England, the possibilities were infinite.

Maybe he went to the cliffs, a short walk from the

house, to watch the light from the lighthouse flickering on the waters. Maybe he went down to the cellar to explore and tried one of the many doors — nobody knew where they led — and got lost in the underground tunnels. Maybe he saw a cat in the park, chased it and got lost on the moor.

The more places they searched, the fewer options they had left. Was there another possibility? They say that when all possibilities are eliminated, what remains is the least plausible one.

They realised that this was not the first vanishing. There was another boy who used to live on this property with his family long ago. There was even talk about more than one child disappearing on foggy nights, never to be found again. All of them just before their seventh birthday.

That makes one wonder why Charly's parents bought this property. Surely they would have heard local rumours about the other children who had disappeared. But it was too late for questions.

They knew that the disappearance must have happened after one o'clock in the morning. After dinner, Charly was safely tucked in bed by nanny Maddie. Later, Charly had a nightmare and cried out like a baby. It was one o'clock when Maddie brought him up a soothing cup of warm milk.

In the morning Charly was not in his room. His parents, his sisters Belinda and Evelyn B, the nanny, and dozens of others, walked the land, the wood, and the cliffs in all directions searching for the missing boy.

Evelyn B was annoyed. At twelve years old, she had better things to do. She was not convinced that Charly was lost on the moor or on the cliffs. Stranger things can happen if you are ready to believe them. There was something else happening here, but she was not privy to it.

In the park she went to the maze. Somebody else had already searched there, but she would give it another go. She looked back at the house. Her mother stood motionless in the door; she looked frozen, both in body and mind. Her boy, her only boy, was lost.

Evelyn B reached the pond. For a few moments she enjoyed the playful dance of the fish. The sun slid on their skin, shiny silver and gold. Her favourites were the goldfish. They used to have a fish tank in the hall, then she and Charly insisted on moving them to the pond — so they would be at large. She was amazed at how they could change their shape and colours.

In the tank, at first, they had had the fantailed ones, dark orange with egg-shaped bodies and silvery floating tails, like the skirt of a ballerina. Those died and their father replaced them. She knew because she caught him with bags with fish.

Charly would ask why they did not grow, and their father explained that they must be a small breed of some sort. Charly wouldn't take that for an answer, so then father would start saying that maybe the fish wanted to stay young, just like father and mother wanted Charly to be their baby boy for ever. He was such a cute baby, their father said. Thinking about it, he never said anything like that about her or her sister. In the pond only one goldfish seemed to be the same: the big one that was Charly's favourite.

One small goldfish came to her. That was strange. They never came to her, but always — absolutely always — to Charly. This one had a yellow body with thin black lines. It was new, probably the latest replacement, and she wondered when that had happened. The fish watched her with one eye; even though it was in the water, it still gave her the pain she got in her soul when she saw somebody crying. She went closer hoping to see a difference. Do fish cry? Do fish look at you? Do fish watch people watching them?

This one was curious. He slid closer to her at the edge of the pond, through the water weeds. It was dumb of her, she knew it, but she felt anxious. The fish jumped out of the water. Was it reaching to touch her face? It scared her. When she pulled back, she fell on her bottom. The gravel stung her really hard.

The big goldfish came up and, with its big shadow, covered the little goldfish. They both disappeared before she could take another look.

She heard a call and ran back to the house. She could swear that those fish were watching her.

That evening Evelyn B could not get to sleep. She felt sad about her missing brother. He must be somewhere scared and alone. She also felt sad about the fish in the pond. And she felt sore all over her body from walking all day long. Charly's nanny brought Evelyn B some warm milk. Nanny Maddie was big; her thick arms were warm when she embraced her. Her apron smelled of yeast and flour. She was always baking something for Charly. After a few sips, Evelyn B's eyes closed, and Maddie took the mug from her hands.

Evelyn B fell asleep with the wind blowing the curtain wildly in the window. She saw Charly, but she knew it must be a dream. In real life, Charly was not made of a white cloud. In her dream, he was sitting on the bedside table and watching through the window a light that was coming from the maze. He sneaked out of the bedroom and tiptoed down the stairs. Evelyn B followed him. The front door was heavy. At the front, the pebbles were loud under his feet; Evelyn B looked around wondering if anybody could hear him. The night felt chilly; she wished she'd taken a jacket. He started to run towards the light, a yellow beam shooting from the moon to somewhere inside the maze. It took him to the pond where he started talking to a fish.

'You want to play with me?' the fish asked.

'I am cold. I should go back in.'

'Come in here. It's nice and warm.'

She was worried about her brother talking to a fish in the middle of the night, yet somehow it was okay. Just one of those things.

Charly touched the water and took the finger to his lips. His face lifted and he smiled happily. Evelyn B was curious, so she also tasted the water. The water was warm and sweet; it felt like custard and tasted like vanilla.

Charly stretched his neck and sniffed. The giant goldfish, a glittering yellow with heavy dark stripes, started to swim up and down in the water, left to right and back. It was big — the size of a cat. It was bigger than she remembered.

'You need to come in. Now,' the huge fish said.

'Why now?' Charly hesitated.

'If you miss the moon rays, you cannot play with me.' He twisted his big belly and pointed towards the bottom of the pond. 'We have games here. Lots of them.'

The boy could see them now. Evelyn B looked in over his shoulder. A castle with a gate and a bridge, stone horses and pawns on a chess board.

The fish swam with his head out of the water.

'Touch my head and you will see things never seen before by humans.'

As soon as Charly touched the fish, his body started shrinking into a tiny goldfish, shiny and silvery. As he plopped into the pond, Charly remembered what he'd wanted to ask.

'What is your name?'

'Gilbert.'

'I am—'

'I know who you are. I have waited many years for you.'

But Evelyn B knew that nobody would believe her dream.

## SHADOW

The Romans had doubled the guards and her raid in the fortress took longer than she had expected. She searched the temple for the Queen's burial, but it was not there.

She escaped the enclosure, but centurions were following her and getting closer. Shadow, her horse, was nervous.

She passed the Lake of the Fairies where the priestesses gathered for the festival of the Goddess Bendis. They danced under the moonlight, dressed like brides. The one who would see their beauty would be blinded, the one who joined them in their dance would die. She remembered the strong smell of the goldenrod wreaths in their hair. It was so long ago! The weight of time felt heavy on her shoulders. All the things that had happened since: the war, the death of their King, and Dacia becoming a Roman province.

Snapped branches interrupted her reverie. She dismounted, whispered in Shadow's ear, then set him free. The horse galloped in the woodland and a few Romans chased after him. The horse would find her when it was safe.

Agile in her leather sandals, the Dacian sorceress climbed towards the peak. From the top she could see the whole valley. Seven well-hidden forts were built in these mountains. The Romans had burnt most of them down. The Queen had been killed and buried in one of their temples.

She heard hooves behind her. Hunkered on a rock, she pulled the hood over her head. Her eyelids lowered over the light of her eyes. With a low voice she conjured the winds.

*Seven winds like seven brothers* — Her limbs got smaller, shoulders dropped and back hunched. She felt pain in her fragile bones.

*Good to know, good to others* — Her skin wrinkled, her hair greyed and twirled like dirty sheep fleece. The time clutched around her heart.

*Flesh to make, years to take; The old Chira-maid to get* — Her mouth became toothless, and eye sockets hollowed. She felt bewildered.

Each verse-spell transformed her body.

'You!' the Roman called.

When the crone turned to face him, the soldier flinched. Her crooked fingers with long black nails held a cloak around the decrepit body. He wanted to ask if she had met a rider with a horse. Her white clouded eyes looked through him. The question was senseless. The soldiers surrounded her suspiciously, but then pulled away. Hastily, they returned to their pursuit of a young Dacian rider.

Left alone, her body struggled to grasp the change. She sat there. Long hours.

She will soon forget where to return, what her other shape was. She will need help to bring back her body from its meander.

She started to forget. She could not remember who she was and where she was.

She could only remember Shadow. Shadow will know. He will find her and help her.

She found a cave nearby. She hobbled to the safe lair and waited for Shadow.

# A COMMUNIST ELECTION,
# SPRING OF 1985

I remember that 1985 was the year of my political protest, because it was the first year my brother could vote.

Spring was warm in 1985 as our small town's communal hall was being prepared for the elections. It was given a lick of fresh paint and a wing was set up as a voting section. The Club, as we all called it, sat on the national road and everyone who drove past it had the privilege of seeing our country's flags, next to the huge, framed portraits of Ceaușescu and his wife, Elena, who called herself an Academician Doctor Engineer. Oddly enough, in those photos they never seemed to age regardless of how many years they remained in power. You could never escape that President; his poster was everywhere, watching you.

The Club was a large grey concrete edifice. The public buildings under communism were intended to shove in as many state institutions as possible. This — our Club — was the local cinema, the local concert hall, and the local library. For as long as I had lived in my hometown, The Club always smelled of old sweat, mouldy paper, and dust that was so engrained in the thick red carpets that you couldn't beat it out of them even if you spent ten years trying. The building was freezing in the winter, and a stinking sauna in the summer, but it was the hub of our town.

Communist elections in Romania were very quick because there was only one party, and that party put forth one candidate: Nicolae Ceaușescu. The Communist Party always won the election. The voter turnout percentage was always high: around ninety-nine per cent. They never said what happened to the one per cent who did not participate, but we all knew that those who had had the guts not to turn up went straight on a Department of State Security blacklist quicker than you could say 'multilateral socialist society'.

That spring I was a teenager, with a teenager's opinions on the regime and its heavy censorship, and with a visceral hatred for the pretence of the election. I couldn't understand why my brother was so cocky about getting to vote — what did he have to be proud of, other than being born at the right time? He only had to show up at The Club, get his name ticked off the list, get the piece of paper with the name of the party and its candidate, fold the paper into four, place a stamp on it, drop the paper into the voting urn, turn around, left foot, right foot, and march out of The Club having discharged his duty as a citizen of the Socialist Republic of Romania.

More than ever before, that spring I felt I could not fit in. The same as most of my schoolmates, my reading list included stories of different times – *The Count of Monte Cristo, Les Mystères de Paris*, and Karl May's novels about the Wild West – and I relished how their protagonists spoke freely, even if it got them into trouble. Most of the time they succeeded in doing something for their beliefs and changing things. And what did we have? We had Radio Free Europe, which we could only listen to secretly, with one member of our family keeping watch at the door to be certain we wouldn't be caught enjoying seditious material by the Securitate or its spies. We had our fantasies about defecting to the West; we entertained stories about people who smuggled themselves out of the country hidden in trucks or shipping containers; we heard stories about people crossing the border on foot and being shot or getting arrested.

I was still a young person, painfully aware of my limitations. I knew I probably wouldn't make it out alive if I tried to defect. I stewed in my own helplessness, and in my disappointment with the elections which made a mockery of a democratic system.

So, in the spring of 1985, I sabotaged the elections.

I brought my sister into the cause. She was thrilled to be party to sabotage, but then she was even younger than I was. We spent the weeks leading up to the election day making various plans, weighing up possibilities, and instilling in each other the keenest sense of secrecy. We both knew what the possible consequences were.

Our plan was simple, and the preparation was easy enough. We raided our father's magazine collection for some older issues he wouldn't miss. We tore off the front pages which showed printed portraits of Ceaușescu. We used woollen winter gloves because of vague concerns about fingerprints. In each of the portraits, Ceaușescu was ruddy faced, plump and smooth, gazing benevolently off the page with the expression of a kindly father rather than a dictator. With shaking hands, we wiped the pages with a towel — meticulously, inch by inch — to clean any fingerprints. With woollen fingers we used the most commonplace blue ballpoint pen we could find and proceeded to deface the portraits; fearfully but emboldened by our just cause, we drew thick-lined swastikas on his forehead or on his cheek.

In the end, we had ten of these prints for our efforts. Our father would have noticed if more of his magazines went missing. We hid the defaced prints and the leftover magazines behind the brick stove in our room.

The night before the election, we were ready. As we lay in our beds and waited for everyone to go to sleep, time seemed to stretch to infinity. In his room, our father was listening to Radio Free Europe and smoking. On her creaky pull-out sofa, our mother was reading one of her cloak-and-dagger novels. 'Just stop fussing,' I thought furiously when we heard her go into the kitchen for her usual late-night snack.

By the time all the lights were off, and the house was quiet, my sister and I were bursting with impatient nerves. In the moonlight that streamed through our window, we gestured to each other and carefully sat up, then began to dress in the black clothes and hats we had carefully stashed under our beds over the course of the week. It's strange how such a small thing as getting ready in the dark can alter your perception; every sound was amplified in the darkness. Every squeak of the bed, every creak in the floor, every rustle of the shrubbery in the garden made us pause for long moments while we prepared. As we finished dressing, we pulled our turtlenecks up to cover as much of our faces as possible. We'd read somewhere that faces shine in the dark.

It must've been past ten o'clock by the time we were ready, with the prints rolled up and hidden about my person together with a stick of glue. In the quiet, the window to our bedroom creaked absurdly loudly. My heart skipped a beat when I imagined our mother waking up and finding us both dressed like burglars. I steeled myself and pulled the window open sharply. Fresh spring air blew in like a shower over our already sweaty faces. We heaved ourselves out of the window and into the garden, crouching low as we dropped, silent and watchful. Before we left, I carefully pulled our window near-shut. My mother was sensitive to draughts.

Our neighbours' gardens were completely foreign to us as we snuck through; every breaking twig and rustling leaf under our feet and hands issued forth a menacing alert. Garden gates screeched like banshees that must've stopped my heart half a dozen times. We walked through back gardens and an empty field, to avoid any streets where we might be seen by passing cars, and we sneaked close to walls and fences away from streetlights. We discovered a town that was alien to us. With everyone in their beds after curfew, the streets were deadly silent — except for the screaming urgency in our chests. We could get caught out in the yellow streetlights, and what could happen to us then?

During the day, this walk took ten minutes, but that night it took over forty-five. We got to the park and slipped into it through a gap in the hedges. We laid on our backs on the grass for a well-deserved break, our cramped calves and bent backs aching from the hunkered-down walk we'd done the whole way. Between the tree branches, we watched the stars and the moon for a while until my sister tapped me on the shoulder, reminding me that we had a job to do and pointing towards the other end of the park. Through the grass and along the well-manicured shrubs, we crawled on our bellies. We had jumped out of the window at night several times before, but those times were for fun, a game or meeting our friends at a campfire. This trip was different. But we thought the hardest part of the night was over; all we had to do was get to the side of the park which faced The Club, cross our town's main road, glue our posters to The Club's solid oak doors, then hightail it home. We were basically done already!

That's why getting to the main road was a shock. As we peered out at it from behind hedges, it seemed twice as wide as it did in daylight, and five times better lit; in short, despite the lack of traffic, the road was suddenly ten times riskier. The Club was also outrageously well-lit for a local community hall during Romania's economic austerity period and, to top it all off, there was a guard. An actual soldier, uniformed and alert, was patrolling around the building. It struck me as ridiculous that there was a soldier guarding the voting section in such a small town for an entirely rigged election. I pressed my face down into the grass, and the soft earth beneath it muffled my groan of frustration. Of course, the communists were prepared. The two of us — stupid, naïve children — had assumed we'd be the only ones thinking of sabotaging this sham and believed that nobody would expect such a thing to happen. To sit and chat about it was not an option because we had to be silent, but our eyes and hands were having a tête-à-tête. We realised that anything could go wrong now: a change in patrol, a car, a late visitor returning home. We could be caught in the shrubbery or in the middle of the road.

We could have given up and turned back there and then … but we didn't. All these new obstacles only proved to us that we had a message that had to be spread, and so our purpose and resolve were fortified. It was also a matter of pride and ambition; were we capable of finishing what we had started? I sat back on my haunches in the shrubbery, rolled my collar down and pulled the hat off for a few moments. I just had to wipe some of the sweat off my overheated face, risks be damned. I took a deep breath of the cold night air and my lungs rattled with the chill. Slightly calmer, I pointed at my watch, then at the soldier, then drew a circle with my finger in the air. My sister understood me.

For the next half an hour, we watched the soldier on his patrol. We counted his steps, noted how long he was visible to us, and hoped against hope that he would be lazy, or slow, or just stop patrolling altogether, perhaps sneak off somewhere to have a nip of plum brandy. But he didn't. He was as steadfast as we were, and each lap around The Club took less than a minute. There was no way we could cross the wide road and the stretch of pavement leading up to the building's façade, put up our posters on the entrance door, and then cross back to safety again. We were bold and brave, but not magic.

Still, we did not give up. It was too important, and we'd already come so far. We just had to reconsider the situation. In front of The Club was the Heroes' Monument Garden, full of rose bushes and fenced by trimmed hedges. I thought about it for a while, and eventually whispered, 'We need to get to the Monument. We've got fifty seconds to get there before he comes around again.'

My sister pointed to The Club's entrance; her own bare face screwed up in doubt. 'But we can't get there.'

I shook my head and said, 'No, we can't.' It was a big blow to my ego and my imagined triumph when people showed up to vote in the morning and saw our work.

Then we realised that we had a second option: the council's notice board. It was closer to the Heroes' Monument and on the path leading up to The Club. People would see it in the morning because they had to walk past it.

'Fifty seconds to the Monument. We stop. We count

his patrol again.' My sister nodded. 'We wait for him to walk to the back.' I pointed to the bulge under my jumper. 'You keep watch. I stick up the posters.'

With one last determined nod, we pulled our hats back down over our foreheads and our collars back up over our noses. We crouched in wait. As soon as the soldier faced away from us, we shot across the road — lightly, with silent footsteps. As we reached the garden across the road and began the crawl under the bushes, my heart began to pump so fast I could hear the blood rushing in my ears. We got into position and waited. From where we lay, fully covered, we had a better view of the soldier. From afar, he looked impressive. Up close, we could see he was a skinny young man who dragged his feet and smoked, probably to keep himself awake and stave off his boredom on a night where he had to be here doing this thankless task. The scent of the cigarette smoke was familiar: rough, unfiltered, stinky *Carpați*, the same as my brother smoked.

We watched him for several more rounds, recounting and gathering our courage. Then I took out the posters and the glue. For a long moment, I stared down at the paper glue I had with me. Why had we thought that paper glue would work on the wooden door of The Club? Why had we thought it would work on the glass case of the notice board? Would this be the reason for our failure? My sister nudged me, signalling that we should get ready. I tried to ease a cramp in my leg without scraping my shoes too hard against the ground.

My mind was overwhelmed by a chain of incessant thoughts: we would be caught, we'd go straight to prison, our parents and brother would be sent to prison with us. I wiped sweat from my eyes, and I caught a whiff of myself. I smelled like fear. The night stretched endlessly under the hedges, as endlessly as the rest of my life and my family's life in one of the labour camps.

But, of course, nothing is endless. Thoughts and fear followed the universal rule, and in the same way as they started, they also stopped.

I handed out the posters to my sister. The soldier's boots sounded on the gravel leading to the back of The Club. I pushed myself up from the ground, rushed out from the bush and took the few steps to the notice board. Hurriedly, messily, I smeared the glue stick across the glass. My sister, kneeling near the board, handed me a poster. I slapped it onto the glass, as perfectly straight as you please. I smeared more glue, plastered another poster next to the first, this one decidedly crooked. I didn't care, just went on smudging the glue on the glass and putting up posters. Wonderful how terror sharpens the wits and makes time fly so fast. Before I knew it, we were out of time. My sister tugged on my trousers to let me know it was time to get back down, and she reached up to press each of the five posters we'd managed to put up, to make sure they were stuck. They were.

We dragged each other back into the garden with the sleeping roses, hearts hammering. She whispered in my ear, 'Fifty-four, fifty-five,' then fell silent. The soldier appeared above us, silhouetted against the sky in the moonlight. He did the round on his allotted patrol while we buried our faces into the grass and waited for our courage to return.

When we finally dislodged ourselves from our spots and made our way back across the road, the young soldier was walking around The Club. We continued counting his footsteps as we left. Our feet carried us home as quickly and as quietly as they could manage.

Somehow, we made it. Somehow, we let ourselves back in through the window. Somehow, no one was waiting for us in the dark of our bedroom. I sat on my bed and watched my hands shake with nerves and exhaustion.

We got into our beds — black clothes hidden

underneath again — as somewhere on the hills the old church bell tolled. Our night of mischief finished at three in the morning.

The next morning, of course, we slept in. We missed our father and brother going out to vote but woke up to their loud voices in the house upon their return.

My brother: 'You should have seen the police commissioner. His face was so red, and he was sweating like a pig in his uniform!'

My mother: 'Who did it?'

My father: 'They don't know. They'll investigate it thoroughly, I'm sure. Can you imagine? Whoever did it will be dead when they find them.'

In the space between our beds, my sister's gaze met mine. We shared looks of equal pride and fear. Our plan had worked. We had achieved something. We had done something meaningful. People had seen our counterpropaganda, and the authorities had taken notice that there were still people out there — even here, in our small town — who would speak what had to be spoken.

I spent the morning in a light-headed daze, floating from my lack of sleep, but fuelled by my ego.

At noon, when our family was sitting together, the news on the radio announced the results:

> *'The victory in the elections of the Socialist Unity constitutes a new and vibrant expression of the force of our revolutionary democracy, the unity of the people, the strength of our socialist society, which under the leadership of our glorious Communist Party, makes its own future, free, with clarity and well-being, the future of our society, socialist and communist ...'*

I slammed the bedroom door shut. The wall around the door frame cracked.

'Sorry,' I shouted. 'It's draughty.'

# THE CALLER'S ALBUM

After all, he had enough time on his hands to devise the game, find the pawns, and set the plan in motion. He found the monotony of his life detestable, and he had to do something about it.

### Linda, the taxation office lady

The street was an urban art scene, the brick walls painted in coloured murals. One of her favourites was in a narrow alley near the Perth Taxation Office where she worked. The mural spread on both sides of a lunch bar.

'Hey. You've been naughty.'

'Carl! You should not call me in the middle of a

working day,' she teased. The blonde woman blushed all the way to her hair roots.

'Who is Carl?'

'Oh. Who is this?'

'Oh. Just a caller. A caller who knows something about a call you made on the twenty-fifth of May last year to a certain office.'

'What do you want?'

'Tzk, tzk. You cannot be naughty today. What do I want? That depends.'

Somehow, she knew that she could not afford to irritate her caller.

'It depends on how much you want to keep your job with the Taxation Office.'

'You are a con. I'm hanging up now.'

She heard a click and then her muffled voice coming from a recording. 'Do you protect whistleblowers? I need to know that if I talk, I am protected (pause). Something that occurred in the Perth Taxation Office. Are you interested? (pause). Briefly? We received a directive to make certain calls. As it happened, some employees in the office called the wrong people and some accounts got messed up (pause). People complained and, conveniently, a lot of data was lost (pause). Later, we said that it was scammers and not the Taxation Office (pause). Yes, I have proof with dates and names.' She heard another click and the recording stopped.

The caller chuckled. 'As you may have noticed, Linda, I also have proof.'

She felt the coffee heavy in her stomach, milk and chocolate threatening to come up her throat. The egg sandwich in front of her — the one that she had been craving since that morning — now looked like a bad monster. She held the phone tightly to her ear, afraid that somebody could eavesdrop. She saw her boss coming into the café and ordering a coffee from the till. He smiled and waved at her.

She asked quietly, 'What do you want?'

'Call in sick now and take the rest of the day off. You need to clean up some mess. Go to see your lawyer and tell him that you withdraw your claim on Mike's property. Take the paperwork to Mike tonight. You will both have signed it by next week.'

'I don't think I can.'

'Oh, but you can, Linda. You have just been promoted and today is the day you should be getting used to your new office. Your first office, away from that narrow cubicle.'

'How do you—?'

'Do it today, Linda, or tomorrow you will not have an office to come back to, or a job for that matter.'

Her mind was already searching for an excuse to take the rest of the day off.

'You can always tell them that the mayonnaise in that egg sandwich was not very fresh,' he chuckled.

She looked around wildly. Nobody was talking on the phone; nobody was looking at her.

'Who are you?' she whispered.

'The caller,' he whispered back.

The line went dead. She was really sick now. She ran to the ladies' and threw up the coffee and the half sandwich that she had already eaten.

### Mike, the cabinet maker

Things happen every day. Weird things, bad things, surprising things, great things, and spooky things. That day, Mike had a strange call which was all in one.

'Hey. You had a problem. A problem that you don't have anymore.'

'Who's this?'

'It doesn't matter. Your problem has been taken care of.'

Mike emptied the baked beans from the can into the bowl ready to warm up his lunch and, holding the phone between his ear and his shoulder, shoved the bowl into the microwave.

'I don't know shit. I don't know what you're talking about, mate. If you don't tell me who you are—'

'Your ex-wife will withdraw her claim for the whole house. You can pay her out as you suggested. I'm calling you to cash in and I'm only asking for one favour.'

The brash words of the stranger sent a chill down his spine. His ex-wife had called him the night before. She had sounded scared and, to his surprise, had told him that she would give up on her settlement requests. He had asked her why, but she didn't reply. And when he dared to ask her for visitation rights for their son — because he liked to push it — she went quiet. For a few long seconds, he expected her to go mad and start shouting at him. Instead, she agreed. 'Sure. Why not?'

And that was it with his ex. And now the caller.

'I hope you haven't disappeared on me, Mike.'

'No. I am here.'

'Do you know why I'm calling?'

'Maybe.'

'You can do better than that, Mike. It's because you've cashed in more than you bargained for. Now it is my turn. Are you with me, Mike?'

'Yeah, mate. Tell me.'

'You will receive a call tomorrow with an address and a service request for a bookshelf. You will accept it. You will do the job, it will be finished on time, and it will be impeccable. When you go in to take the measurements — and this must happen tomorrow — be prepared to find a way to make copies of all three keys on the chain. Put the copies in a ziplock bag and tape the bag under the bench in front of Gosnells City Council by tomorrow night at midnight.'

The caller took a break while Mike was processing the information.

'I hope I do not need to undo the things that you got resolved with your ex.'

Mike answered, maybe a bit faster that he intended to. 'No, it's okay. I'll do it.'

'Good. You can return to your lunch now. Baked beans today, is it?'

'Who—?'

The line went dead, and the baked beans were forgotten in the microwave.

### Mary, the nurse

Fremantle hospital was quiet. The carpark was usually full — mostly because of the road repairs and repaving of the carpark in progress — but at eight in the evening it was almost empty. Mary tripped on one of the orange cones and muttered a curse. Her phone rang while she was standing on one leg rubbing her ankle.

'How are you today, Mary?'

'I'm good. How are you?'

The caller could not stop himself from playing cat and mouse.

'Just be careful with those cones. If you fall, you may break something.'

She looked around. It was dark and, as far as she could tell, the carpark was empty.

'I don't have time for hide and seek, Mary. I need you to do something for me.'

'Sorry, who is this? Is this Jeremy?'

'No, it is not. Unless Jeremy asks you to steal drugs for him.'

She gasped, hung up and started to run towards her car. The phone rang again before she opened the door.

'A fast reflex you have there, Mary. But that won't wipe out the records of all these fake prescriptions.'

For the next thirty seconds her phone beeped with messages. She opened two attachments.

'Are you there, Mary? And please do not ask me who I am. It gets tedious.'

'What do you want?' she whispered, getting in the car. She felt better behind locked doors.

'I need the real stuff, the best stuff, and I need thirty grams.'

'I am not sure if I can.'

Her phone pinged; messages with attachments kept coming.

'Okay, okay,' she shouted.

'You are feisty.'

'So? What are you going to do about it?'

'Nothing. As long as I get what I want. Delivery must take place tomorrow night at midnight. You must go to the Supreme Court Gardens in the city. It will be on your way home. Put the drugs in a ziplock bag and glue it underneath the kangaroo statue that's drinking water.'

'Who are you?'

'Oops. You just couldn't stop yourself. For you I am… the caller.'

He chuckled and hung up.

**Jim, the freelancer**

The rain was pouring angrily but it didn't deter the shoppers. They ran the few steps from the car to the gazebo near the entrance to Bunnings. The smell of fried onion and barbecued sausage welcomed them; almost everyone stopped to grab a sausage sizzle and a drink.

Jim was dressed in his overalls, ready to do some work for a client after he'd bought the materials. He could not resist the sausage temptation, but as he took his first huge bite, his phone rang.

'Jim Barnes?'

'Yes,' he mumbled with his mouth full.

'If you wish to stay free, you do what I say.'

He froze with the roll in the air. 'Who is this?'

His question was ignored. 'Take another bite of your sausage and just listen.'

Jim choked, but the caller kept talking.

'If I'm going to save your arse, you will have to do me a favour. When you go home, you will find a set of keys and a piece of paper with an address on it. They are in your box under the floor where you keep your tools.'

Jim wiped his mouth with the back of his sleeve. 'Who the hell do you think you are? How did you get into my living room?'

'Try not to interrupt. It's rude. You will go to that address tonight at ten o'clock sharp. The second door on the right is the office. Behind the desk there is a safe. Inside you will find one sealed brown envelope. Take it. You have under an hour for the job, so don't waste time and don't touch anything else. Drop the keys and the envelope in the rubbish bin in Mary Carroll Park at midnight. The new bin near the picnic area, across the lake.'

'You are joking, mate. And if I don't?'

'Let's not waste our time. If at midnight the envelope is not in the bin as requested, the police will receive an anonymous call and your house will be searched. They will find a ziplock bag full of pills — you know which ones, the prescription ones. I left a couple of pills as a sample in your toolbox. Only I know where the others are in your house, but the police dogs will find them. Like I said, I am saving your arse. If I get what I need, I will tell you where they are and you can have them for yourself. A win-win case, eh?' Jim was silenced. 'I must hear that we are on the same page here, Jim. And don't forget your tools tonight. You might need a drill.'

Jim threw the remaining sausage in the bin, together with the unopened Coke.

'Why are you doing this?'

'Finally, somebody with an imagination. I've never had that question before.'

The caller hung up.

### Robert, the philanthropist

'You will have to end your holiday, Robert.' The deep voice came through a voice modifier.

'Can I help you with something?'

'The sun hasn't burnt you and the mosquitoes haven't bitten you so far on your holiday island. It's better to leave while you still have some nice memories, or before bad things start to happen.'

'Who is this?'

'The caller.'

'I don't know you.'

'You don't need to. You only need to know that I have some interesting photos of you and your son, James. You know which ones.'

'I don't have a son.'

'You sound like a petulant child. Yes, you do, Robert. You may not want to hear about him, but he is still your son. You can hear about him from me or you can read it in the newspapers.'

Robert took his drink from the table and walked away from the pool.

'Why are you calling me?'

'Because you have something that I am interested in.'

'I won't be blackmailed.'

'It is not blackmail. It's a trading agreement. If we consider the huge effect that these photos would have on your anti-drugs charity work…'

Robert wiped his palm on his linen shirt and took a sip from his cocktail.

'This is what is going to happen. The photos of you and your son sniffing white powder will be sent to a few chosen newspapers tonight. They will be on the front pages tomorrow. Or I can stop that from happening.'

'What do you want?'

'A smart question.' The caller was amused. 'I want one painting from your collection. I am not greedy. Only one. The painting by the unknown artist. They think it was one of the first convicts in Fremantle prison, don't they?'

'How do you know about this?'

'Tzk, tzk. Wrong question, Robert. You may keep all the other items in your collection, even though we both know quite few of them were illegally obtained.'

The silence was interrupted by a sequence of photos being sent to his phone: his house, his garage, his vault, and a few items from the collection. Robert wondered who had betrayed him to this extent. Finally, two photos of him and his son, grinning in front of the desk in his study, on which could be seen thin rows of white powder. Photos that he knew should be in his office safe; photos for which he had paid a lot to get back a few years ago.

'You can choose to stay there for the next two weeks — you know, finish your holiday. I will take care of the rest. The story about your party style and your collection will be sent to the newspapers.'

'Okay. Enough.'

'This is how we do it. You take the four o'clock flight back to Perth. You pack up the painting in the paper and the cardboard box that is waiting for you near your garage door. At midnight you drop the package into the rubbish bin behind the yoga studio in Subiaco. You know it.'

'How do I know that you won't contact the papers?'

'Well, you don't know. You'll have to take my word for it. The proverbial honour amongst thieves. Once I have the painting, I will return the photos. All of them. This was great fun.'

He hung up.

### Checkmate, the accident

He had wanted the painting since the very first time he saw it, drunk and high at Robert's party. To be fair, he only really wanted it because it was Robert's and he wanted to take something valuable from him – after everything Robert had taken from him. There were so many other ways he could have arranged for this to happen, but none of them would have given him the same thrill. He had enjoyed finding people to do the dirty work for him and pulling all the strings. That reminded him: he had to call Jim back and let him know the hiding place for the pills. He had probably turned his house upside down by now.

The caller indicated to go left and, when the light was green, pulled out onto the crossroads. At the last second, he noticed the truck speeding through the opposite red light.

He pressed the brakes abruptly and heard tyres screeching. The sound was followed by a rumbling of crushed metal in his right ear and all around him. From the corner of his eye, he saw the side window smash. For a short while he lost consciousness; when he opened his eyes, he felt totally in the wrong place. People were shouting at him: asking him if he could hear them, asking him his name. He had an unbearable pain in his arm. His face pressed into the rugged upholstery of the passenger seat. It smelled of coffee. He had done that; he had spilled the coffee just over a week ago. He looked down at his right arm. From below the elbow, the arm was missing. Blood spurted. He wanted to cover the chopped end, but first he wanted to know where the missing arm was. They would need it at the hospital to put him back together. He looked at the dashboard. The last thing he saw was his hand holding tightly onto the wheel.

Everyone thinks that you won't feel or know anything anymore, but the mind always finds its way through. He did have the chance to realise he was dying.

When the ambulance came, they declared him dead at the scene.

When the police came, they found his identification and recognised the surname of a prominent man. They called the Chief of Police and he called the victim's father. When his father arrived, they let him go to the car. Robert, the philanthropist, found a big flat parcel on the back seat. It had been squashed and broken in two by the power of the collision. Robert slowly peeled off the corner and started to reveal a painting of a wide corridor and — as he expected — a row of doors, which he knew belonged to the main cell block. The painting, in faded colours of brown and yellow, was the work of art of an unknown artist, one of the first convicts in Fremantle prison.

# UPAVISTA KONASANA

Millie had been going to yoga classes for months now because she wanted to understand what she needed to do to get rid of her cravings. It was quite an effort for her.

She never made a booking, just showed up at a time that suited her.

The studio was always set up for the Yogis. Twelve mats were laid out in three rows of four. The props that they could use during the practice were stacked up next to each mat: a folded blanket, two foam blocks and a perfectly curled strap.

Millie always took an empty spot right up front, almost

in line with the teacher's huge round mat. She wanted to watch him closely. She always took in his body while he was stretching and lengthening his limbs. She was fascinated by his toned arms and his fingers dancing in the air. She was so close she could almost see the pulse through the vein on his neck.

At the end of the class, as she lay on her back trying to relax in the Corpse Pose — Savasana — she felt ridiculous and wearied by new sensations that she did not want to admit.

She stayed behind to complain.

'I still don't feel any different. It's not helping me. I cannot relax in the Corpse Pose.' Only she would know that was a lie.

'Are you practising meditation?'

'No, not really. Should I be?'

He looked at her openly, directly, with worry visible in his eyes. His brown eyes were lively and shaded by impossibly beautiful long dark eyelashes that every woman would envy. He wanted to convince her not to give up.

'I am here earlier most days. Maybe you could come fifteen minutes before the class and we could do some breathing exercises. It will help you to relax.'

A few days later, she approached him again. 'I have changed my mind. I am not coming anymore.'

'You should be patient with yourself.' His voice was soothing and deep, having kept the warmth of the final minutes of relaxation.

'I cannot relax. I am very tense.'

She was having a bad day — as in, a seriously bad day. One of those days when she questioned every decision that she had ever made in her life. The yoga teacher had to take the brunt of it.

When she had decided to take up yoga, it was because life was not giving her enough space. She could not sleep, she could not find her place, and her urges were becoming irritating. She was depressed and she did not trust doctors.

The teacher insisted, 'If you really want to see a difference, you need to be committed to it. I believe that your flexibility has improved.'

All she could think about was his body. Very fit, very good muscle tone, and the uncovered forearms pulsed with the veins that popped out due to intense workouts. He looked so sweet she could barely stop herself from tasting him.

She shook her head and pursed her lips.

'I am not sleeping any better.'

His strong passion for the subject was visible in his vivid eyes. 'Yoga helps to reduce stress levels and gives you better posture and balance. Sometimes you see it as an overall improvement, and other times you see it in certain things.'

'I don't know what else to do.'

She stopped going. The handsome yoga teacher texted her to ask if she was all right. She messaged back to say that she had a back pain and wanted to take a break.

But her desires became even stronger.

One Monday evening, she went back. In one corner there was a huge salt lamp; it was the only source of light in the studio. Incense was burning in a wooden box with holes in the lid, and the aromatic smoke rose in the air in a straight column. White sage was the generally accepted scent, the most neutral one. That Monday, though, it was sandalwood — a smell associated with religious shrines — and Millie hated it. She needed all her strength to stay for the practice.

The theme for that night's class was hip opening. The teacher explained the need to open your hips and said the postures can create an energetic shift. Yogic tradition holds the hips as a storage ground for negative feelings, especially emotions related to controlling one's life;

opening the hips can help release those emotions. As Millie watched him spread his legs wider than she'd ever seen a man do before and lean forward into the space in front of him, she almost missed the posture's name: Upavista Konasana.

After class she watched him while he put the props away. The fantasies almost took over entirely. She had to be careful ... or maybe she didn't. With her back against the shelf that was loaded with mats and blankets, she tried to hide a yawn. He stopped what he was doing and turned to face her.

'I know they say that yoga "supposedly" helps.' She raised her hands in the air and drew quotation marks with her fingers. Her nose twitched, and the corner of her lip pulled back.

'What do you mean "supposedly"? This is not one of your anti-ageing face creams that you keep trying, not knowing if it will work or not. You need to allow your mind to connect with your body.' He regretted his outburst almost immediately.

She shook her head and lowered her voice to a mumble. 'For me, it's not working.'

She curled her palms in frustration. In her closed fists, long nails started to cut into her palms. There it was again: the corner of her lip pulled back and upwards. Inside her cheeks there was a pressure as if the space inside her mouth was getting smaller and tighter. She hiccupped in a last attempt to hide it. The teeth growing and sharpening could be quite an intense feeling.

Around her heart the temperature plummeted to extremely low; she was freezing, and she needed to do something about it.

'What exactly is it that you expected from yoga? What is your concern?' he asked, taken aback by the sneer on her face.

She waved her hand to push away the smoke from the

incense box. She opened her fists and her sizeable claws seemed to enjoy being let out.

'You delicious fool.' Her smile would have looked cheerful, if not for the teeth. 'I had expectations. I was hoping it would help.'

A wider smile and two fangs poked from underneath her lips. She sensed the warmth coming from her hips — recently opened, of course — as they released her pent-up emotions and created a fire in her lower abdomen.

His dark eyes widened in stupor as her claws seized his neck. Her lips came closer until he felt the breath hot on his skin.

'It was my craving for blood I needed help with,' she hissed into his ear, but she was not entirely sure if he heard it. His blood was already dripping off her lips.

# MARISA LAKE

On the top of the mountain, the castle stands silently under the clouds of rain; its turrets lose their shape in the mist, and its blind windows are swallowed by the rain. The wide alley that leads to the arched entry gate is smothered by vegetation. The count had left his Transylvanian castle just before the legends started to unfurl.

He said he wanted to leave the disease behind.

'What disease is that?' they would ask.

'Too much love,' the count would answer.

Travellers give up looking for any sign of life in the fortress and continue along the muddy road, letting themselves become captivated by the lake: a land of fairy tales, a place where the water and the land meet in one magic connection. Twice a year, in the spring and then again in the autumn, when rain falls heavily, the lake overflows its shores and transforms the place. The old trees are buried half in the water, the sun blinks through the naked branches in colours of green and flickers of yellow, and the fish slide gracefully between the trees.

The village is bordered on two sides by the shores of Marisa Lake, and on those shores the wild horses spend most of the year. They call it the Horse's Village, even though the shore is also alive as a home for foxes, wolves, birds, and snakes. After many floods over many years, the villagers have been forced to move further inland, abandoning the shores to the horses.

The foals wander through the deserted old borough of clay houses with their collapsed porches and brown-rusted tools still hanging on the sheds' walls, until a worried neigh calls them back into the fold near the lake.

Legend has it that Marisa Lake is treacherous, and those who dare to roam there alone, and let the dark find them on its shores, are found with two puncture wounds on their neck.

When the traveller finally cuts themself from the charm of the lake or the grace of the horses, the track will widen into a road that leads into the inhabited village. The visitor's attention is drawn to the first house on the left, with a beautifully carved gate, and its door and window frames painted in a bright blue. The horses often come as close as to graze over the fence into the orchard at the back, as if they are still trying to push the villagers further and further away from the shore.

For days now, the autumn rains have been falling. In the muddy courtyard, children are calling for a girl to come out and play. The creaking of the door is followed by a woman's hearty voice. 'Make sure you are back home before dark! You don't want Marisa to get you.'

'Yes, grandma!' Agapia means it.

She remembers the boy who one evening stayed behind to watch the horses. They found him the next morning in the lake with bites on his neck.

Agapia is joining her friends when, all of a sudden, the air is filled with a rhythmic sound. She shushes them and the children stop in their tracks. She squats and presses her palms on the soft ground. She can make out a reverberation coming from afar, the pulse of the hooves hitting the ground. Her eyes look into the distance. They are still far, but she wants to welcome them. She stands and runs through the orchard, trailed by the calls of her friends. Rain is soaking through the canopy. Almost breathless, with rain in her hair, she comes out on the other side near the shore.

She holds her hands out to the rain, the spell of the sky that is bringing the horses to the lake. The green oasis will become the horses' home and she has come to watch them.

The herd finally gallops out of the forest. With their skin glistening, they slow into a canter and nicker excitedly while checking the shore and the dry areas where they can shelter from the rain. Agapia recognises a colt from the previous year; his long legs of pure white look slim on his brown-red body. He comes closer and neighs at her when she holds out her hand, then playfully turns and runs back to the herd. From afar, just hidden behind some bushes, she watches the foals fool around, and tries to make out who is the alpha mare. She observes life inside the herd, the moving bonds between the old and the young. Kingly animals with a mysterious life, and yet so much in common with people. As she sits there, watching the horses playing and greeting each other, she loses track of time. Just before dark, she races home.

'The horses are back at Marisa Lake, grandma.'

'You know you should not go there.'

'I just peered from afar, grandma.'

After dinner, Agapia is not ready to sleep.

'Tell me the story, grandma.'

'It is not a story to tell.' The old woman knows exactly what her granddaughter is asking for.

The girl's dark eyes are curious about everything the world can show her. She brings her palms together in a prayer. 'Please, grandma. I will feed the chickens every day.'

A candle is lit on a stool. The old woman sits on the bed, tidies her headscarf around her chin and, with a whisper of a voice, starts to speak.

'Marisa was a beautiful girl. Her father, a rich boyar, was away when his castle was attacked by a band of outlaws.'

'Was it the castle in the mountain? On the other side of the lake?'

'Maybe it was, or maybe it wasn't. The tale goes far, and nobody knows for sure.' She frowns at her granddaughter. 'And if you interrupt my story, it shall come to a quick end.'

The girl tightens her lips shut, and the old woman carries on.

'Marisa was at home with a few servants. The outlaws stole all the riches they could find and took Marisa and the servants as prisoners. They took her to their chief. He made her his woman, and he loved her beauty so much that he could not see the sadness in her eyes. One night Marisa could not live with the shame anymore. She ran away.'

The girl gasps as her grandmother continues.

'Dressed only in her nightdress, she ran through the forest. She kept running, hurting her bare feet, scratching her arms and her face, but she did not feel the pain. She ran and ran until she reached the water. Back then they called it the Big Lake. She fell on her knees at its shore, and she knew there and then how she could be free from shame. She walked in the water, all the way in, until she did not feel anything anymore. The outlaws searched for her all night, and the next day they found her in the lake. Her face was still beautiful, with her alabaster skin. On the neck she had two small bites.'

The old woman pauses and wipes Agapia's tears.

'Yes, the chief of the outlaws was sad too. He lost her and his heart never healed. So, he spent the rest of his life on the shore of the Big Lake, and he renamed it: Marisa Lake. He saw her many times, dancing on the shores in her white nightgown. They say he might have found his end in the same lake. Nobody knows all the story or what happened afterwards,' the old woman finishes in a low voice. 'And now you will close your eyes and go to sleep.'

She blows out the candle.

***

Agapia goes to see the horses every day in the next weeks. One day she follows an old man with woollen trousers, a linen shirt, and a leather belt heavy with tools.

The old man carries a long piece of wood to the water where a mare is lying down and seems to be hurt. The man drags the wood under her back legs which are almost in the water. He himself is half in the water, and he stays there and talks to the mare in a soft voice. Agapia realises the mare is foaling. The other horses are just watching them from a distance. The man waits with the mare until the foal comes, then the mare stands and takes the foal to the herd. The cold twilight embraces the lake as Agapia leaves the horses to settle for the night and heads home.

'It is dark, child.'

'Not really, grandma. It's just started to get dark.' Then she adds thoughtfully, 'Maybe the old man knows where Marisa's castle is.'

'What old man?' Worry etches the grandmother's

eyebrows.

'I am sorry, grandma. I followed him to the lake. He helped a mare that was foaling there.' She quietens, waiting to be scolded, then asks, 'Do you know this man? You know everybody in this village. He carries a belt with lots of tools.'

The old woman sighs and starts to plait the girl's hair for the night. Her fingers touch a lump behind her granddaughter's right ear, and a chill wraps her heart.

Her fingers search again, hoping it had just been her imagination. But it is there: a faded scar of two small marks. She finishes plaiting her granddaughter's hair and the girl lays her head on the pillow.

'So, do you know who that man is?'

The grandmother rests her warm hand on Agapia's forehead. 'Sleep, child. The night is late.'

'Grandma?'

'Yes, child?'

'I am cold.'

The old woman puts another blanket over the duvet and blows out the candle. The moon lays a yellow light over them, and the light seems to dance as the old woman starts to talk.

'It was another autumn when the horses came to the lake. We had a big storm, with a wind that banged madly on the wooden shutters. The gate was creaking on its hinges, and the water — oh, I had never seen so much water pouring down. I never have since. Then the rain slowed down, and the thunders quietened, and we could hear frightened neighing coming from the shore. In those days, there was a boatman in our village. He was the only one who went to the shores. He went out that night, too. A mare was foaling, like the one tonight. A while afterwards the neighing stopped and then the rain stopped, but the boatman did not return.'

She holds her jaw tight to stifle a sob. 'The lake finally

took him. Like all the others. It was the last time I saw him, walking through the pouring rain and lit up by the thunder. My man never came back.' She sighed. 'You see, my child, that boatman was your grandad.'

In the dimness, the old woman comes closer to look at the girl's face. The story is lost on Agapia; she has been long taken by a deep sleep. Her chest rises slightly with the resting breath.

The tears find their way down the old woman's ridged cheek, their warmth shielding the scar from the cold when her lips touch it. She tucks the duvet around her granddaughter's tiny body.

'There, there. The nights might be cold for you, child.'

She wonders when Marisa will call Agapia to be with her. Hopefully, not yet. When that happens, at least Agapia will join her granddad and she will be with her beloved horses.

Soon.

# THE FLOOD

A shrill voice, tinged with fear: 'What do you want me to take?'

A rough, deep voice: 'Just warm clothes and blankets.'

It was her mother and father. Maia woke up slowly, lingering between oblivion and consciousness. Something cold brushed her face. Had the window been left open last night?

From in front of the house, more voices broke through her dreamlike state. She opened her eyes. Unearthly yellow beams like mystic reflections danced on the walls and filled the room with ghosts. The rain hit the roof in heavy resounding waves.

Maia had to see what was going on. She sat up on her bed and the bedroom revealed itself in dark shapes and shades. Hurriedly, she stripped the blanket away and placed both feet on the floor. She squealed. So cold! Right up to her ankles!

The water covered the floor, wall to wall, like a moving carpet. As if taking a cue, her father entered the room, wading through water. In a few long strides he was next to her. He lowered his flashlight and put the metal box that he usually kept in his desk on the bed next to her. Then he grabbed her under the arms and lifted her to stand on the bed. She was fascinated by the high gumboots he wore and his bright yellow raincoat. Surrounded by shadows, she looked up at his long face; his steel blue eyes were fixed intently on her.

'I know you're strong, and you won't cry.' She tried to look behind him into the dark, but he blocked her view. 'Right?'

Her mother arrived and quietly handed Maia her boots and a raincoat.

'We need to leave. We need to get ready,' her father whispered, as if not to bother the ghosts. Soggy story books and stuffed toys floated listlessly on the menacing surface of the water. Maia worried that water would find its way into her mother's boots, because of her shorter legs.

'Maia, look at me,' her father commanded. His hand squeezed hard on her shoulder. 'Can you be a big girl now? Can you be brave for me?'

Maia nodded. He helped her pull the boots on, then he put the metal box in a satchel which he hung across her shoulder. 'This box belonged to my father. It is everything I have left from him. You look after this. The satchel will just hang here, and no one can know what's inside,' he said, helping her into the raincoat. Then he picked her up and carried her out of her bedroom. In the living room the water had risen under the chair seats. She buried her face in the crook of his neck; he smelled of cologne and cigarettes. With her forehead she could feel his vigorous pulse — so close that she thought she could find her way into his heart, and from there share his fearlessness and determination.

'Remember how we tried to see how tall you are if you sit on the fence?'

When Maia didn't reply immediately, he craned his neck to look at her.

'You're not afraid, are you?' She shook her head. 'I need you to tell me so. Can you speak? As far as I know, you have a very sharp tongue!'

Her head snapped up. 'Of course I can speak!'

'Good. You know we've had a lot of rain lately. Well, this is called a flood and for a little while we will be wet. Just like when we go to the river and walk in the water. It's just water. Nothing to worry about and help is on the way.'

Outside, the rain immediately washed over her face, and water sloshed aggressively around her father's legs. She tightened her arms around his neck. She felt strong in his embrace. Most of their neighbours were outside, in front of the barracks. Maia's father put her on the fence, wiping the water off her face with the back of his hand.

'Hold yourself on the fence with both hands,' he instructed, placing her feet on the lower beam.

She gripped the damp wood tightly, finding her balance. Her father looked around.

'Not everybody came out,' he said, then called out, 'Itzik! We need to go and knock at every door to make sure everyone knows about the evacuation.'

He turned back to Maia and covered her hands with his palms. 'I'm going to go and help the others. You keep still. I will be back in a few minutes.'

She dared a slight turn of her head to the left. Her best

friend was sitting on the picnic table in front of their house. Maybe she was not strong enough to sit on the fence like Maia — and she was crying too. Baby!

On the main alley, a truck was slowly advancing through the water. Its white lights swept over the building and the sodden faces of their worried neighbours. The long, flat building appeared smaller because of the water.

Her mother approached her carrying blankets, the water slowing her down. She looked at her daughter reassuringly.

In the lights of the truck, a thin silhouette near the fence caught Maia's attention. Maybe she'd imagined it. The water carried away a stuffed cat, then a book, then a shoe. Was that Angela's tennis shoe? Maia thought the red shoelace might be familiar. She saw the dark figure again, moving behind the truck, away from everybody else. She whispered loudly to her mother. 'Mum, I think somebody is there.'

Her mother squinted through the drizzle. 'It's nothing. Just shadows.'

Maia was watching people getting into the truck when her father returned. 'It's your turn to go in the truck.'

'Do I have to? I want to stay with you.'

'Okay. I will take your mother first. She needs to help the neighbours with the baby. I will come back for you and take you last.' He smiled.

Her mother kissed her knee. Maia pushed her long black hair away from her face and tried to sound confident. 'I'll be all right, mum.'

While escorting her mother to the truck, Maia heard her father say, 'The water has risen twenty centimetres in the last half an hour. I am not sure if we will get another truck down here. After this one leaves, everybody will have to walk up to the main road.'

When her mother had climbed safely onto the truck, Maia heard her father call to one of his workers. 'Marcel!

Where are you?'

'Here, Sir. Boss.'

'Go to the police quarters and search for constable Titi. He is on duty for emergency. Tell him that everybody needs to be evacuated to the highest ground in the village, right near the general store.'

The man made a move, then hesitated. 'Do I have to go to the party committee?'

Maia's father grunted. 'They can wait. Right now, we have better things to do than to keep the communist commissar informed. Go!'

The man turned without another word and disappeared into the night.

They heard a neighbour calling for help and her father waded towards them.

The truck, crackling its gear box, drove away with its load. The lights disappeared and left the barracks in the hands of the overflowing river. The night hummed with rain. Suddenly all alone, Maia could feel the coldness of the night.

The water rose, pushing against the fence and making her dizzy.

A small man with mousy eyes approached her. She didn't recognise him, but he could have been one of her father's workers.

'Do you need help with the bag?'

Maia pulled her raincoat shut. This could've been the person she saw hiding behind the truck. 'What bag?'

He pointed towards her arms. 'It must be heavy. I can help you.'

'I'm fine.' She shifted on the fence, trying to move further away. The cramp in her calf gave her a good jolt. She shook her leg, but she began to slip off. The man moved closer with his hand outstretched, ready to grab her. As she prepared herself to shout at him, it happened. Her fingers went stiff on the slick wooden fence and into the freezing water she went with a whimper. She pushed herself up in the murky water and moved towards her house, her body soaked and heavy.

'Oh my God, girl! Let me help you.'

Maia didn't trust him. 'No! Go away! I'm going into the house to get my mother.'

'You know your mother left with the truck.'

She shook herself free and took a few steps into the house.

'You'd better leave. This is not your house,' she yelled, hoping somebody else would hear her.

The man looked around and followed her cautiously. 'But I want to help you.'

'No, you don't. Get out. I don't need your help.'

He tried to grab her again, and this time she bit hard on his hand. She heard a yelp and a stifled curse. She turned and tried to move faster. The water went up to her knees as she struggled onwards, through the hallway, through the living room. She looked around wildly, trying to find something she could use to protect herself and the box. The carving knife from last night's dinner lay on the table. She grabbed it, wondering what she could do with it. She hoped just the size of it would scare the man. She moved towards her bedroom and lifted her heavy leg up the step.

'Where are you going, girl? Don't be stupid. Let me help you.'

She turned to see the man right behind her, standing in the doorway. She stretched her arm out with the knife.

'Don't come any closer. Go away!'

The man laughed. 'What are you going to do with that? Shave me?'

She moved back in the water and the mousy man tried to follow her. He tripped on the step, lost his balance and collapsed on top of her, grunting angrily. His weight pushed her under; she swallowed water and her nose burnt. Her left hand held the box tightly to her chest. She lost the knife and struggled to escape from underneath his body. She finally wiggled out and raised her head above water, inhaling deeply. Still coughing water, she dragged herself away from him and struggled to stand. If only somebody would come for her. But there was nobody. She was by herself.

She saw the storage cupboard, half opened, and she knew it went all the way under the bed. She had always called it 'the cave'. In the dark, maybe he would not see her going in. As she heard a splash behind her, she crawled — almost dived — into the cupboard and deep into the gap. At the last minute, she decided to leave the door ajar. She hunkered down in the water with her back against the wall and closed her eyes. The water now reached her neck. She half expected to see the man's face in the door. Instead, a waterlogged teddy bear barely floating — poor teddy.

There was another splashing movement in the water, then stillness settling in. Maybe he had given up on finding her hiding place. How long would she be able to stay hidden there? Half an hour? An hour? Her father had said that the water had risen twenty centimetres in half an hour. How long would half an hour be? How much would twenty centimetres be? They never teach you that, do they? Maybe they would find her later, in the cupboard with her teddy, and she would be floating like that tennis shoe. Would she drown here? Maybe if she slept, time would pass faster. She was tired; she wanted to sleep. But she knew she shouldn't. She had to keep her chin lifted to breathe.

There wasn't much time left. Maybe if she took a few sips, just a few, there would be less water? The water dripped from her hair and the muddy smell engulfed her. Her fingers grasped the box, her skin slippery and creased, and her body was stiff from the freezing water. She allowed it into her mouth, then spat it out. It actually didn't taste that bad, like … fish. She took another sip and spat it out again. Only her face broke the water, and her neck hurt from being bent backwards. She swallowed the next sip of water with frozen lips. Her face had no more space for air. She could only drink. She could try and hold her breath. For how long? She could sleep. Go to sleep.

'Maia, where are you?'

It was her father's voice. Was she asleep already? Was she dreaming? Her body quivered. She heard splashes.

She tried to shout and then choked. Every noise was muffled by the water. She moved too quickly and took another sip the wrong way. She started to cough.

Her father's strong hands grabbed her through the water and dragged her out of the cave. Her arms were still clamped around the box. Shivering, she looked around. 'That man wanted the box.'

Her father scooped her up. Water dripped off her clothes and a water-filled boot slipped off her foot.

'You hid there? You could have drowned.'

'And let him have the box?'

She saw the mousy man in the water. Floating face down.

'What is wrong with him?'

'I think he is tired. I will send somebody to take care of him.'

Once again, he carried her out of the room.

'Do you know what is in the box, Maia?'

'No.'

'Then … why?'

A whimper from behind her frozen lips. 'Because of what you said.'

'What?'

'You told me that this is everything you have left from your father.'

He blinked a few times. 'Maia, do you want to see

what is in the box?'

She nodded with chattering teeth.

He took her into the living room where the chairs were floating around the table. He stood her on the table, put her boot back on, then opened the box. From inside he took a velvet pouch, spilling its contents into the box. Maia's eyes widened. Glittering diamonds, big gold coins, and gold pocket watches — like the ones she had seen in the old photo of her father's grandfather at a family wedding. With frozen fingers, she touched them with a sense of humility. Then, she gently placed them one by one back in the pouch and closed the lid.

'Your father loved you very much. He left you all this treasure.'

He hugged her until she felt breathless, and then took her out of the house again. 'Do you think you can last one more minute on the fence? I need to find someone to go into the house and take care of that man.'

Her face was a block of ice, but she clenched her jaw and nodded. He put her on the fence and brought a dry blanket to wrap around her.

Maia felt on top of the world, up on the fence, with her grandfather's treasure box safe in her hand and the dark water surrounding her.

Her body was cold and drenched all the way through, but somehow it felt like a summer's day at the river. It was just water. Nothing to worry about.

And that was that. Behind the barracks, the sky slowly lit up. The sun rose as it did every other morning.

# THE TRUTH BEHIND THE FEAR

You saved my life that day, and I will always be grateful to you for that. I did not trust you before, but that day you proved me wrong.

We never know what the truth really is, do we?

It was an autumn day, perfect for a walk. Your face soaked up the sun and your eyes gleamed. You have this thing — everybody can see it in your step — about how you carry yourself: you exude joy.

My Fitbit showed that I needed two thousand more steps to reach my target. It was one of your good days and it was my chance to show you that it's all right. So, I suggested a stroll in the park.

Once in the park, I talked about my dream, and you listened. I blabbed, and you listened. My dream was about a woman who moved her belongings around in a dark alley. Something weird. What else? You know, one of those dreams from which you wake up with a bad feeling. But my dream was just a way to distract you.

I knew about your fear of the dark, so the more the sun went down, the more I talked. When the dusk started to settle, I was nervous for you.

I struggled so much in the years since you came to live with us. You lost your mother and your brothers; I knew there were some things in your past that you wanted so badly to forget and things that you could not express.

I was so frustrated with you. I wanted to dispel the fear that made you lash out then hide away for hours. I felt hurt by your recoil when I hugged you. I thought that love did not need a book, did not need words … surely everybody could feel and understand love?

I was taken aback by your anger. I tried all I could. I smothered you with love, with kind words, then I shouted at you, and I punished you when you were mean. I gave you nice things, trying to buy your love. I wanted so much to see you happy that I refused to see that bribery was not the right way. I failed each time.

Then your fears shifted to me. You jumped when there was a sudden knock at the door, and I jumped with you. You hid when there were steps outside on the street late at night, and I hid with you. You had a nightmare and cried in your sleep, so I went to wake you up. I wanted to comfort you and reassure you that you were safe. You looked at me with blank sleepy eyes and I sometimes saw hatred in there. I know that you did not believe me, and it hurt me. I cried in frustration, not understanding what I'd done wrong and what I was supposed to do to help you.

I am sure I dreamt about lonely, frightened women because of you, because of the pain I could see in your eyes. Will I ever be able to find out what it is, the heavy pain in your soul?

So, we walked in the park next to each other, and I kept going on about my dream. Then, from the corner of my eye, I saw that you were not there anymore. I looked back and I noticed you were hiding behind me, as if away from the dark.

Your eyes were narrowed, your neck stretched, your chin lowered. In your fear, and how you held your breath, I could almost see in you a lion prowling.

Then it happened. From behind a tree, a man jumped out and attacked me with a knife. Before I had the chance to process it, he grabbed my arm and brought the massive blade under my chin. I smelled on him alcohol, and filth. I forced my head back; I struggled to create as much space as possible between his knife and my neck. I froze and I did not dare to draw breath.

'Give me the—' was all he had time to say.

You jumped from behind me, and you snatched his wrist. Your quick movement pushed me back, and I lost my balance. You growled with a rage like I had never seen before in you. You bit his arm hard and you shook it in your jaw. The man screamed. He dropped the knife, but you still did not let go.

'Call off your dog!' my assailant shouted.

I stood up and took the time to clean my trousers, then I touched my neck to make sure that his knife hadn't cut me. And then I watched you, and I smiled, and my heart grew amazed at the beauty of your strength and the loyalty of your heart. You were still on top of him, and there it was, I could see it again. Your ears were pulled back, your body tensed, your neck lengthened and your head hanging down. Your teeth held on to the man's hand. The hand that had tried to hurt me.

That is when it clicked. It was not fear for yourself that I saw in you. You were prowling — prowling for the dangers that could hurt your master. It was not fear that pulled you back, it was you getting ready for attack. You were in full protection mode.

So, yes, that day you saved my life. From now on, my dear dog, I will always trust you.

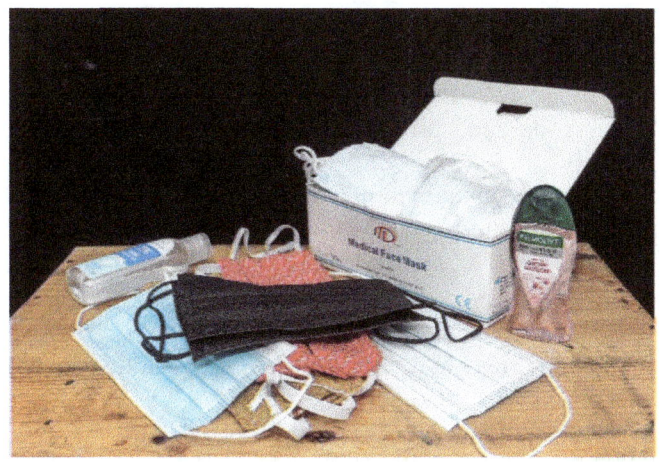

# THE WORLD AT A STANDSTILL

Once again, the world is at a standstill.

The silence rings in your ears. You try to hear if there are any cars out on the street. It seems they have all faded away. The sun is out all right. It will be a peaceful, hot day.

Silence is placid today, encircled by absence of motions.

The neighbours are noiseless. Nobody walks down the alley. The builders across the road have not turned up today — unless they have found a way to work silently.

Silence plummets over the houses, over the streets, like a wrapper tight around a candy.

The wind has gone, too. Vanished into the quietness.

You strain your ears, trying to hear the yapping dog from two houses down. The ringing of the silence becomes almost ear-splitting.

You pick up a distant hum. Maybe it is a car in the distance. Or the train. No, it's gone. Maybe it was just a creation of your imagination. Both the creation and the imagination fade away. They leave behind a painful stillness.

One noise comes from another part of the house. You can hear the cheap clock tick-tocking with every move of its hands.

The calmness comes from everywhere — waiting, expecting something to happen. Or not.

On the Friday before Anzac Day, in Perth, two people tested positive for Covid-19.

This is why the city is in lockdown again.

This is how mornings start in lockdown.

At a standstill.

# FOR THE REST OF HIS LIFE

The years following his death were an empty, silent time. Not until I was ready to remember did the days slowly begin to fill with my father's tales of life.

The image that flashes through my mind now is his hands: big hands with long, elegant fingers that held the baked potato on his plate steady as he scooped out the middle — softened with butter and sprinkled with cheese — then lastly, folded and ate the skin.

He used to call it 'the feast'.

He had a story about potatoes, and I believed it. I believed every single word because I grew up with this story. It was a story that father would nonchalantly bring up whenever we, the children, were fussy about food. I remember only snippets from his story; it always felt incomplete. But over the years I have learned enough to fill in the gaps and re-tell the story of a prisoner of war.

Father spent more than two years on the Russian front — only a few months in battle, and the rest in a labour camp in the Russian steppe. But I should start at the beginning.

In 1944, Romania had already lived through four years of German occupation when the government decided to join the invasion of the Soviet Union, and the Romanian Army was forced to fight alongside German troops against the Russian Army.

The war found my father on the Northern Moldovan frontline, close to the border between Romania and Russia. On the twenty-third of August 1944, a coup took place in Bucharest and a new government was formed. Romania switched sides and the Romanian Army was instructed to lay down their weapons.

Father told us that it was a cruel irony for him to be taken prisoner 'on the last day of the war' as he called it.

I allow myself to imagine what he must have seen on that memorable day, when the guns and cannons stopped spewing their projectiles. How despondent the battlefield must have looked in its quietness. Were there bodies strewn over the field, and rifles and helmets that had lost their owners? Was the air of the hot summer's day infiltrated with the smell of blood and gunpowder, and the cries of the wounded? Were the flies buzzing around without taking notice of the sheets of paper blown in the wind from the communication trench?

We can imagine it how we want, but the fact is that soldiers with the Romanian Kingdom coat of arms dropped their weapons, walked out of the trenches, and raised their hands. And my father was among them. He was not yet twenty-three years old, and probably felt relieved that the war was ending. They had expected to receive new orders to continue to fight alongside the Russian Army. Instead, they were loaded into trucks, then herded onto cattle wagons and taken deep into the Russian steppe. Their destination was a labour camp and from then on, my father was a prisoner of war.

He painted for us a picture of a camp where they were put to work rebuilding bridges and roads in Russia after the destruction of the war. Upon their arrival, they were asked if they had ever worked in construction. Father had studied to be a construction engineer and he was good at it, so this was his opportunity.

For most of my life, I knew him hovering over construction plans and inspecting the work on the construction yard. But there, as a prisoner, what was he thinking? And how did he work?

He mockingly recounted a time when they took him to a hangar filled with machines that German troops had left behind in their retreat; the Russians had no idea what they were for. Father showed them how to use the machinery for digging and other operations.

He told us there was never enough food. The Russians seemed ill-prepared to feed the large number of prisoners. There is a difference between 'never enough food' and 'starvation', and my understanding is that starvation was the usual state of prisoners there; it decimated them.

He told us they used to dig out roots, and they tried to catch anything that moved for food. I try to imagine how hungry they had to have been to have done that.

I think I heard the potato story a hundred times. They were moved to a camp near some agricultural land. He recalled the excitement when they found out that potatoes were still in the ground, the enthusiasm when they dug them up. Then prisoners and Russians shared the potatoes, boiled with their skins on. Their captors were suffering the same misery. My father remembered it was the only real meal they had during those years. As kids, we always thought this was a happy story from his captivity days, and now I see it differently. If that was the only real meal, how bad could the others have been?

When he talked about the winter in the Russian steppe, he described it as the kind of cold that went all the way through to the bones and lingered there. Yet he still felt he was one of the lucky ones; at least he could see the sun.

He lived those years with the hope that the Romanian Army would come back for them, especially after they heard that Hitler was dead. He must have been mad with impatience.

On the other hand, I believe that he must have learned about patience in those days. I remember his calm nature and positive attitude in front of any problems. He was a wise man, and it took me years to make the connection between his experiences as a young adult and his character as an older man.

In his second year in the camp, father got ill with malaria. He shivered when he described the chills and searing, mind-numbing pain, and the complete weakness that followed. He had a strong fear for the rest of his life of being bedridden.

One day, he found the Russian camp commander playing chess alone. The chess board had many pieces replaced with odd objects. Of all the places in the world, a labour camp was the place where father became friends with a Russian colonel. They both spoke French, and between the building plans and their love for chess, they spent a lot of time together.

If it were me, I would have been full of anger and hatred, but father only saw that both captor and prisoner missed their families. They shared the hunger and the cold steppe and the long games of chess.

My favourite part from his captivity story was how it ended. By the autumn of 1946, father had been a POW for more than two years.

One day the colonel came in his military vehicle to find my father on the construction yard. In a terrible rush, he asked father to get in the vehicle and then sped off. Then he delivered some news.

'A train is coming and will stop near the hangar for a short time. I will take you to the bottom of the hill. From there, it's up to you. The shortcut is directly over the hill.'

At this point of the story, father would lift his arm and point somewhere in the mid-air in front of him. He always, without fail, lifted his arm as if he was the colonel. He painted a vivid image for us — and that was because of how strongly he remembered that day.

'There is a chance you can catch it,' the colonel had said as he stopped the car. 'Run and don't stop until you get there. We don't know if a train will ever stop in these parts again.'

Father hesitated between disbelief and fear until the colonel pushed him out of the car and shouted. 'Just go! This is the run of your life, Nestor!'

He ran. He only looked back once to see his friend waving at him. That run, he used to tell us, gave him the true meaning of the words 'run for your life'. He also said that although he never had the time to say 'goodbye' or 'thank you' to that man, he remained in his thoughts for the rest of his life.

He ran. He fell and got up, his body ached, his lungs burnt, but he refused to think what would happen if he missed the train. He did not stop until he reached the hangar. The train lines were barely visible between the tall grass. The place was deserted, and he thought he'd missed it. He thought that was it. Exhausted, he struggled for breath and coughed, ready to spew his lungs. Despair brought tears to his eyes.

Then he heard a train whistle. He lay low until the train had overtaken him, then it stopped. He sprinted to the last wagon, pulled the door open, threw himself on the filthy floor. Very soon, the train began moving. During the journey, father lost count of the days, between fever and unconscious sleep. Death hunkered in every corner but refused to take him.

When he woke up from his final sleep onboard, the train had stopped, and he was a short distance from the Romanian border.

He got home.

He brought the malaria with him, and at home a good doctor treated him with quinine. But the captivity and the disease had left him in a bad state. In his photos from those days, his face and body are emaciated; I used to think it was because of his smoking, but now I know it wasn't.

The actual liberation was in the summer of 1951, but many Romanian POWs were not released before 1956.

His recount was undoubtedly vague. He did not tell us too much from those two years in captivity, and I believe that he carefully crafted out the most unpleasant bits. It was more horrible than that. I know it was. There was always something behind the words, or between the images, something missing that should have been there to complete the picture.

But he lived to tell the tale.

And I can see him, with the eyes of my mind: a scrawny, breathless figure standing on the top of the hill, at dusk. It must be dusk because the darkness of not knowing follows. But for my father the darkness would never be the same, and he would never fear the unknown. He survived it once.

# ACKNOWLEDGMENT

My heart is bursting with millions of emoji hearts and thanks, to my daughter, Raduca, for her time and patience, for the shoulder always there in need, for her criticism and approval, for editing and proofreading, for ideas and suggestions.

My *minune-dragă-scumpă* – miracle-darling-dearest – is what I used to call her from her first days in this world, long before she even understood the meaning of these words. She remained the same and more and this journey was just like another delightful page in the book of our memories together.

Her support during this journey called 'writing a book' was invaluable and I could not have done it without her.

Whenever I was stuck on something, I reached out to her. And she was there.

Whenever the world spoke to me, I asked for her help to hear it.

I am grateful to my son, Raul, for his help with the book cover. His ideas came at the right moment, and he approached the challenge with commitment, taking the photo that would become part of the book cover.

I would like to express my appreciation to my husband, Ivan, for his understanding and immense patience during the extra busy days when writing was my priority.

I would also like to express my thanks to Cristina Grigorescu for allowing me to use her painting for the book cover.

I would also like to thank some teachers from different

stages in my life: Maria Danciu, James Parsons and Dr Deborah Hunn, for their classes and guidance. They made it look easier.

My deep thanks to my editor, Georgina Gregory, who did a tremendous job editing my stories, being inquisitive when my Romanian way of thinking did not fall so easily on the pages. Her positive encouragements meant a lot to me. My thanks as well to Hilary Mudditt as the extra pair of eyes that worked on proofreading my stories.

# ABOUT THE AUTHOR

Maria Grigorescu was born in Romania at an unmentionable point between 1960 and 1970, and lived there until 2006, when she moved to Australia.

Throughout her working life, she has worn many hats: mother, bookkeeper, yoga teacher, administrative manager, dental nurse, catering business owner, electronics technician, secretary. Her favourite hat, however, is *writer*.

She lives in Perth, Western Australia, with an extremely tall husband and a dog.